NETBALL GEMS

netball
AUSTRALIA

Hooked on Netball
Chase Your Goal

A Random House book
Published by Penguin Random House Australia Pty Ltd
Level 3, 100 Pacific Highway, North Sydney NSW 2060
www.penguin.com.au

Penguin
Random House
Australia

Hooked on Netball first published by Random House Australia in 2015
Chase Your Goal first published by Random House Australia in 2015
This omnibus edition first published by Random House Australia in 2016

Addresses for the Penguin Random House group of companies whose addresses can be
found at global.penguinrandomhouse.com/offices.

National Library of Australia
Cataloguing-in-Publication Entry

Creator: Gibbs, Lisa, author
Title: Netball gems bindup 1 / Lisa Gibbs, Bernadette Hellard; illustrated by Cat MacInnes
ISBN: 978 0 14378 088 5 (paperback)
Subjects: Netball – Juvenile fiction
Other Creators/Contributors: Hellard, Bernadette, author. MacInnes, Cat, illustrator
Dewey Number: A823.4

Cover illustration by Cat MacInnes
Cover design by Kirby Armstrong
Typeset in 15/20.7 pt Adobe Garamond by Midland Typesetters, Australia
Printed in Australia by Griffin Press, an accredited ISO AS/NZS 14001:2004
Environmental Management System printer

Penguin Random House Australia uses papers that are natural, renewable and
recyclable products and made from wood grown in sustainable forests. The logging
and manufacturing processes are expected to conform to the environmental regulations
of the country of origin.

NETBALL

netball
AUSTRALIA

GEMS

Hooked on Netball

Written by **B. HELLARD** and **L. GIBBS**
Illustrated by **CAT MACINNES**

RANDOM HOUSE AUSTRALIA

Chapter One

Maddy's heart began to pound as she looked up to scan the carpark. She felt her thick brown ponytail swing as she moved her head.

Where is Prani?

Prani was Maddy's best friend and she'd said she would be at training. But training was about to start and Prani wasn't anywhere to be seen. Maddy began chewing on her bottom lip and fiddling with the soft frayed hem of her navy sports shorts.

Come on, Prani! Where are you? I'm going to be the only one without a partner!

'Passing drills! Let's get started!' said Janet, the coach, as she walked briskly up and down between the pairs of girls like a sergeant major. She was tall and wore her long dark curly hair in a messy bun.

The rest of the team began to spread out on the court and prepared to throw chest passes, but Maddy remained where she stood, clutching a ball against her stomach.

Maybe one of the others will pair with me? thought Maddy.

She looked hopefully to her friends from school, Lily and Sienna, but they had already teamed up and made a pair. Maddy eyed the other girls in her team. Training had only begun a few weeks ago so she didn't really know them very well yet. Phoebe always seemed distracted and Maddy had no idea what she was like.

Charlotte seemed quiet. Isabella seemed easygoing. Jade seemed bossy and sometimes just not very nice. In the first training session she'd made some comment about Prani being Indian, which Maddy didn't get. What did it matter?

Now what? Maybe I should go and ask to be a third person for the passing drills . . . But I don't want to be annoying . . .

Maddy's mind raced.

What if the coach takes pity on me, the leftover girl, and asks me to do the passes with her? That would be the worst . . . Come on, Prani!

The seconds stretched on and for a moment, Maddy wondered why she'd even joined the Marrang Netball Club Under 13s team. Although they were officially known by their club name at games, it had been Maddy's idea to choose a special name for their team. They had chosen the Gems after the Australian team, the Diamonds.

Janet aimed a questioning look at Maddy but just as she opened her mouth to speak, a car with a broken muffler weaved noisily along the track between the gum trees, towards the carpark.

Prani leapt from the car and ran towards the courts, waving madly at Maddy. Her thick black braid bounced, and her earrings glittered in the late-afternoon sun.

'Sorry I'm late –' she began.

'Quick!' interrupted Maddy. 'We have to start or we'll miss practising chest passes!'

They found space on the court and stood about two metres apart. As they began their chest passes, they heard the coach's clear voice.

'Now remember, everyone,' Janet called, 'when you catch a chest pass, you grab it with both hands, one on either side of the ball. I want you to grab it strongly and hold tight, like a two-year-old who grabs and says "Mine!".'

Instantly, four pairs of girls began imitating

a two-year-old with every catch. 'Mine! Mine! Mine! Mine!'

Maddy realised that the idea had worked. She was more conscious of pulling the ball strongly and decisively towards her each time she caught it.

Relaxed now that Prani was here, Maddy began to enjoy training. They moved from chest passes to bounce passes. It reminded her of the NetSetGO training she'd done when she was younger. NetSetGO was how she'd learnt the basic skills and rules of netball.

The trick to these kind of passes was to figure out where the ball needed to bounce so that it could be neatly caught by your partner, in front of her body. You also had to work out how much force to put behind your pass. If the pass was too strong, it would bounce too high. If it was too soft, it would bounce too low, making it difficult to catch.

Prani used the right amount of force but her aim wasn't that great because she was distracted, telling Maddy all about why she was late. Maddy lunged sideways to catch Prani's crooked pass.

'So anyway,' Prani continued, 'Nani wanted to start teaching me how to cook, but Mum said she had to wait until after netball training. They talked on and on and on and *on* about it – and *that's* why I'm late!'

Maddy laughed. Prani often talked about her funny grandma, who she called 'Nani'.

The team shifted to practising lob passes. Maddy stepped forward on her left foot and carefully lobbed the ball just high enough for Prani to do a standing leap and stretch her arms high to catch the pass. Maddy's quick, sharp passes contrasted with Prani's loose, fluid movements. Maddy relished the feel of the new netball in her hands. Now she'd be ready for any type of pass in Saturday's game!

Chapter Two

Janet was an experienced coach. She was Lily's mum but never showed any favouritism; she was always fair. She expected the Under 13s team to listen at training and not to muck around. Maddy didn't mind that. She knew that there was heaps to learn, and she desperately wanted to be as good as the older girls in the club. She had seen them training after the Under 13s sessions. They seemed to know how to do everything easily, and they worked so well as a team.

'Okay, question time.'

Janet was about to quiz them. She kept training sessions moving with a range of drills on core netball skills, but she also tested them to see what they remembered. She always said that netball was as much about the mind as the body.

'What fraction is the court divided into?'

Hands shot into the air.

'Thirds,' Isabella called out.

Janet continued to shoot questions at the girls, checking that they all knew the answers.

'Where are the Goal Shooter and Goal Keeper allowed to go?'

'What is the Wing Attack's job?'

'How many steps can you take with the ball?'

'Charlotte, I haven't heard from you yet: what is "contact"?'

Charlotte went bright red in the face and

stammered a reply. 'W-When someone bumps you?'

'Yes, that's right. You can't trip, push, hold onto or lean on anyone from the other team, or make any other physical contact that would interfere with their game.'

When Janet was happy that the girls were learning all the rules, she moved on to goal practice for the day.

'Today we're going to practise the correct goal-shooting position. You all need to know this, because you will each have a turn as Goal Attack and Goal Shooter. Does anyone know the best way to stand and position your arms with the ball?'

Phoebe raised her hand hesitantly. She was tall and slim, with grey eyes that rarely looked straight at anyone.

'Okay, Phoebe. Take this ball and stand as if you were about to shoot a goal.'

Everyone watched Phoebe take the ball and pretend to get ready to shoot. Maddy couldn't believe it.

She looks exactly like a professional goaler! she thought.

'Phoebe, that's perfect!' said Janet. 'Okay, girls, I want everyone to take a ball so I can see how well you're positioning yourselves.'

For the next few minutes, the rest of the team tried to get a feel for the correct shooting position. Each girl stood with her feet apart, her arms stretched out above her head, the ball resting on one hand and the other hand on the side to guide it.

'That's great, everyone! Sienna – feet apart a bit more. Good. Now, here's the important part. You need to remember to bend your knees *before* you release the ball – and then . . .' Janet released the netball she'd been holding. '. . . Aim high in the air, as if you were shooting into the goal ring.'

It felt so unnatural at first that the results were awkward and messy. Charlotte sent a wonky ball up into the air and it landed squarely on Sienna's head. Sienna staggered around in dramatic death throes, sending her teammates into fits of giggles.

'Yes, yes, great death scene,' said Janet. 'Come on, now, time to go find a goal ring – you can use any of the free courts – and have a go. Don't expect to get it right straightaway, though. Just try to get a feel for it.'

Maddy and Prani raced to the goal post at the end of court three. Prani tried the position and aimed the ball at the goal ring. The ball didn't even make it high enough to reach the ring!

'This is hard!' she exclaimed.

But Maddy wasn't watching Prani. Her gaze

had been caught by Phoebe, who was practising at the other end of their court.

'Hey Prani, come and look at this. Phoebe's really good! How come she can do it so perfectly already? She's 12, the same age as us . . .'

Both of the girls stood still and watched Phoebe shoot with her body perfectly positioned. She bent her knees slightly, just as Janet had told them to, then sprung up. The ball sailed straight through the goal ring! Phoebe caught the ball before it hit the ground, repositioned herself, and shot again. Once more, the ball went straight through the goal ring.

'Wow,' said Prani.

'Yeah, wow,' Maddy agreed. 'Okay, give me a go.'

Her first few attempts fell short or wide of the goal ring, but after a while, Maddy managed to hit the goal ring and, finally, after many, many tries, she got two through in a row!

Maddy was so absorbed in what they were doing that she was surprised when Janet called them back together.

Great! thought Maddy. *Time for game play!*

She raced over with the other girls to where Janet stood, between courts one and two. Maddy couldn't wait to hear which position she would be playing in the practice match.

But she quickly realised that Janet wasn't wearing a whistle. Nor was she holding the position bibs. Instead, Janet was looking down at a large bag at her feet, which had the Marrang club logo on the side. When everyone was gathered around her and the voices had subsided, she smiled up at the girls.

'Today is the day you get your netball uniforms!'

Prani grabbed Maddy's arm and squealed in excitement, and all the girls rushed forward, eager to be the first one to have her uniform.

Janet held up a hand and the girls stopped their playful pushing. 'You'll have to be patient because I need to make sure you get the right size.'

Maddy and Prani grinned at each other. Finally! With their own special uniform, they would feel like proper netballers.

'You know what we need to do now, don't you?' Prani whispered to Maddy.

'What?'

'We need to get ribbons!' Prani giggled. 'Matching ribbons!'

Maddy laughed. 'Yeah, pink ones!'

When Janet called Maddy's name, Maddy raced forward and took her uniform. Waving goodbye to Prani, she hurried over to her mum, who was leaning on the bonnet of their black car, talking to Sienna's mum.

'Mum, look!' Maddy held her uniform out carefully, in both hands.

Maddy's mum straightened up. She had the same long brown hair and athletic build as her daughter. 'Ooh, nice! I like the side panels with "Marrang" written in pink.'

Maddy's eyes shone with excitement. She let the soft, silky drapes of the short dress slip lightly through her hands. The contrasting royal blue and pink colours of the club shone in the fading sunlight.

'I can't wait to wear it to our first game on Saturday!' Maddy said, giggling, as she climbed into the car. She couldn't stop grinning as she clutched the uniform and inspected every single centimetre of it.

They backed out of the carpark and drove along the dirt track that wound through the gum trees and around the football oval, before turning onto the main road in the direction of home.

'Now remember, don't lose it. We can't afford to replace it,' Maddy's mum cautioned.

'There is *no way* I will ever lose this uniform. It's so awesome! Besides, how could I? I'm going to wear it all day on Saturday, and won't take it off till I get home!'

'Okay, okay. Although, I guess if you *did* lose it, you could always wear *my* old netball uniform. You know – the pleated wrap-around skirt with the velcro waistband. Gorgeous!'

'No way!' said Maddy, laughing.

Chapter Three

On Saturday morning, Maddy tried to hide the smile lurking at the sides of her mouth as she walked into the kitchen. She busied herself filling her drink bottle, wondering how long it would take for her dad to notice that she was all ready for netball in her new gear. She could feel the soft cushioning of her brand-new runners hugging her feet as she walked. Her netball dress hung loosely from her shoulders, and her bike shorts fit snugly underneath.

'Woohoo! Look at you!' her dad called out, when he finally glanced up from reading the newspaper.

Maddy did a little twirl for him.

'Now, you know I'm driving you in today,' Dad said, standing up from the table, 'but I can't stay for the game.' He grabbed the keys and the container of orange quarters he'd prepared for Maddy and the team.

'You ready?'

'Ooh, wait! I just have to get my ribbons,' said Maddy as she dashed to her room and back. 'Prani will kill me if I forget to wear them.'

Maddy followed her dad out to the car. She knew he was only dropping her off on his way to quote on a building job. But suddenly she realised that this meant she'd have to walk in on her own. Where was she was supposed to go when she got to the courts? What if she couldn't find her team? She was starting to feel jittery and didn't like the feeling at all.

I wish Dad was coming in with me, she thought.

But Maddy was lucky. When the car pulled into the carpark next to the courts, Maddy saw some of her teammates clustered straight ahead, behind court four.

Tap, tap, tap.

Maddy started at the sound of someone knocking on the car window. It was Prani, standing waiting for her with a cheeky smile.

'Prani!' Maddy exclaimed as she jumped out of the car. 'You're not late!'

'I know. It's a miracle!' responded Prani, and they both laughed.

Maddy said goodbye to her dad and then ran with Prani over to her teammates. As they approached, they heard Jade's confident chatter.

'I've been practising goaling and I'm getting really good, so I'll probably be Goal Attack today,' she said. 'Hey,' she continued, when Maddy and Prani had joined the group, 'we've all got new runners.' She looked closer at Maddy's. 'Where did you get *those*?' she muttered, smirking.

'From the market,' Maddy replied uncertainly.

'Yeah, I thought so,' said Jade.

Maddy looked at the runners the other girls were wearing. Her heart sank as she realised that they were all wearing big-name brands and hers were just plain. Compared to theirs, her new shoes looked ugly and stupid. Maddy felt the smile drop from her face. She looked around at the others but no one seemed to have noticed what Jade had said. They were all talking among themselves.

Maddy turned away from Jade, who had started to boast about how many goals she had scored in her practice session, and walked to the side of the court. She sat on the bench. The warm breeze whipped flurries of leaves and rubbish around her ankles. She smoothed her bright new uniform over the top of her thighs.

As she sat, her eyes wandered over to some of the older girls, who were busy doing their pre-game training drills. They were throwing long passes to each other and made it look so easy. Maddy wondered if she could ever play like them.

They probably have the right runners to play in, she thought glumly.

But then something caught her eye: she noticed that one of the best players in their team had the tattiest, dirtiest runners she'd ever seen. And yet when she took off after the ball, she was so fast that none of the other girls seemed to be able to keep up with her.

Seeing this made Maddy smile. She didn't care anymore what Jade thought. She would run her fastest and show Jade that having the best shoes didn't change her speed one single bit.

'What's up?' Sienna said, bouncing over.

'Nothing! I'm ready to play!'

Then something occurred to Maddy that she hadn't yet thought of. 'I hope Janet doesn't start me on the bench . . .'

Chapter Four

There were eight players in their team but only seven a side were allowed on the court for each game – which meant that someone from their team had to sit on the bench. Sienna and Maddy fixed their eyes on Janet as she moved through the group of girls, handing out position bibs according to her plan for the game against Sandy Bay.

'Here you go, Maddy,' Janet said, handing her the bibs for Wing Attack.

'Thanks!' exclaimed Maddy. She was so excited to be playing in the first quarter of the first game that she barely noticed what position she had been given.

'Now remember, everyone,' Janet said loudly, once she'd finished handing out the bibs, 'you're going to be playing different positions in each game, so think about where you can and can't go on the court.'

Maddy was too preoccupied to listen as she attached the bib to the four velcro squares on the front of her netball uniform. Next she tried to twist her arms behind her back to attach the other one.

'Here, I'll help.' It was Sienna. She came up behind Maddy and patted her on the back to secure the bib in place.

As Maddy turned around to say thanks, she realised that Sienna's front 'GS' bib – Sienna was playing Goal Shooter for the first quarter – was on upside down.

'Hey, your bib's upside down!' Maddy called out, as they walked onto the court.

'Just matching the one I did for you!' Sienna called back.

'What?!' Maddy shrieked, and she burst out laughing – just as the whistle blew and the game began. Maddy tried to concentrate but the giggles were still tumbling out and she couldn't resist looking back to see if Sienna was laughing, too. She was so preoccupied that she didn't notice Phoebe tap the ball away from the Sandy Bay Wing Attack towards her! It bounced off Maddy's arm and was quickly snatched up by the opposing team's Wing Defence.

'Oh no!' Maddy gasped in horror. She looked across at Janet and saw her frown of disapproval.

Trying to make amends, Maddy raced after the Sandy Bay Wing Attack, who now had the ball. She ran around in front of her, took a step back and threw her arms up to block the pass. She remembered the defensive drills they'd done with Janet the previous week. She really hoped this worked.

Brrrp! The whistle blew shrilly.

'Offside,' the umpire called out.

Maddy looked about, wondering who was offside.

'Wing Attack, you're not allowed in this third,' explained the umpire kindly.

Maddy looked at the Sandy Bay Wing Attack and waited for her to move – but everyone was looking at *her*.

'Marrang Wing Attack, *you're* offside.'

Finally it dawned on Maddy that she had run too far and had gone into the third of the court that was out of bounds for her! She had

been so distracted that she had broken one of the most basic rules of the game, one that she'd learnt when she'd first done NetSetGO training! She felt her cheeks burning red as she walked back over the line, into the centre section of the court. She watched the ball being handed to the other team for a free throw and felt sure that everyone was still looking at her, blaming her for making such a silly mistake.

Sandy Bay quickly fed the ball into the goal circle and as Maddy watched the Sandy Bay Goal Shooter score a goal, it occurred to her that Janet may take her off at half-time if she kept making mistakes like that. She couldn't let that happen. She *wouldn't* let that happen. She would show the coach that she could do better. *And* she would show Jade that having special shoes counted for nothing.

'Don't worry, Maddy, next one's ours,' said

Lily, smiling at Maddy as she trotted back to the centre circle.

Maddy smiled gratefully, then took up her position on the transverse line next to the Sandy Bay Wing Defence. The transverse line divided the goal third from the centre third. Maddy stood facing Lily, who was standing in the centre circle. Maddy bounced on her toes, ready for the centre pass. As soon as the whistle blew, she raced forward in front of the Sandy Bay Wing Defence, so that she could be clear for a pass from Lily. But Lily's enthusiastic throw went way too high and threatened to soar over Maddy's head! Maddy leapt up into the air, her arms and even her fingers outstretched, and just managed to snatch the ball down. She grinned in excitement as she felt the ball securely in her hands, and bent her knees to regain balance as she landed again.

'Throw it to me! Throw it to me!'

Maddy only had three seconds to pass the ball. She looked towards the shouts coming from the outer ring of the goal circle. It was Jade, who was playing Goal Attack. A satisfying thought flashed through Maddy's mind – Jade didn't seem to care about Maddy's shoes now! Her hands were stretched forward, demanding the ball after Maddy's perfect catch. But Maddy could see two Sandy Bay defenders rushing forward to cover Jade. She looked for another teammate who was free and saw that Sienna, who was playing Goal Shooter, was standing alone right under the goal ring. Maddy passed the ball long, then watched with her eyes lit up as Sienna turned and smoothly popped the ball up through the goal ring.

Skipping back to her starting position, Maddy ignored a huffy glare from Jade. With a thrill, she heard Janet's voice call loudly from the sideline, 'Well done, Maddy. Keep it up!'

This was fun!

For the rest of the first quarter and the second, too, Maddy concentrated on playing Wing Attack as best as she could. She remembered that she was only allowed in the centre third and all of her team's goal third except for the goal circle – which wasn't actually a circle at all, but a half-moon shape encircling the goal post, where only the goalers and goal defenders could go.

One time, though, she was running so fast when she got to the edge of the goal circle that she lost her balance and fell in!

Brrrp! The umpire's whistle went again for offside and the ball went to the other team for a free throw. This time, though, Maddy didn't feel silly. She had been trying really hard and had just lost her balance.

'Bad luck, Maddy,' she heard Janet say from the sidelines. 'Next time.'

Maddy also worked hard at centre passes. She knew it was her job to try to get out in front of the other team's Wing Defence to take the centre pass from Lily, and then to help Lily get the ball to Jade or Sienna so that they could do their job and score goals for the team.

It was difficult to remember all of the rules but Maddy didn't let it bother her. Running down the court, she felt like she was flying.

Chapter Five

At half-time, Maddy ran straight to the oranges on the bench. She peeled the lid off the plastic container and offered an orange quarter to each of the girls in her team. Sienna immediately put one in her mouth, gripped it with her teeth and gave a wide orange smile. The other girls giggled and followed suit.

'Okay, everyone, over here, please,' Janet called.

The girls hurried over.

'Great teamwork, Gems,' she said, once everyone had settled down. 'For the next half, I want you to focus on coming out in front of your player *before* you call for the ball. I've seen a few of you calling for the ball when you're actually being blocked – and I know you're just caught up in the excitement of the game, but we don't want to accidentally pass the ball to Sandy Bay! I'm also going to change your positions to give you a chance to try something else.'

Isabella leapt forward, eager to take to the court after sitting on the bench for the first half of the game. Maddy pulled her bibs off and waited for Janet to say where she'd be playing for the second half of the game.

'Sorry, Maddy, could you sit the second half out, please?' asked Janet as she handed the Wing Attack bibs to Isabella.

Maddy stared at Janet in dismay. Hadn't she played well enough?

As the girls filed onto court, Janet turned and saw Maddy's face.

'Maddy, don't worry. Everyone will get some time off court this season, it's just the way it goes. Besides, now that you're here, I can tell you how well you played! You know, there were a couple of times there when you reminded me of the other Madison Browne.'

Maddy looked at Janet, confused.

'Didn't you know?' Janet asked. 'One of the players for the Melbourne Vixens is also called "Madison Browne". She plays for the Australian Diamonds as well. Although,' added Janet, 'she's married now so she's Madison *Robinson*, not *Browne*. She looks a bit like you, too.' Janet smiled.

Maddy's eyebrows shot up in surprise. Her mind started racing and she barely watched the rest of the game. All she could think about was what Janet had told her.

When the Marrang Gems won, Maddy got up from the bench, hurriedly shook the hands of the Sandy Bay players, and raced to the carpark to find her mum.

'Mum! Guess what?' she blurted out as soon as she jumped into the car.

'You won!'

'Yes,' said Maddy impatiently, 'but there's something else, too!'

'What? Something more important than you winning your game?' She gasped in mock horror.

'Janet told me there's a Diamonds player with the same name as me! She said that I even look like her!' Maddy added proudly.

'Oh, that's right,' said Mum. 'She plays for the Vixens too, doesn't she?'

'Yes, that's her! Do you think we could go and watch her play sometime?'

'We'll see,' said Mum.

Maddy grinned and settled back in her seat, thinking about how envious Jade would be if she knew Maddy had a double on the Australian side.

Maddy grinned and settled back in her seat, thinking about how envious Jade would be if she knew Maddy had a double on the Australian side.

Chapter Six

It was a week later and the Marrang Gems had just finished playing their second game of the season. All throughout the game, the wind had gusted around the exposed courts, making it difficult for the players to be accurate with passes and shots for goal. Maddy hadn't really noticed the wind so much, as she was playing Goal Defence and was busy chasing the Barton Goal Attack around. But when the ball had been up the other end of the court and she wasn't concentrating on moving about, she had been aware of the wind blowing her ponytail madly about her head. She'd been thankful that she didn't have to try to shoot goals in this weather. She watched helplessly as Charlotte and Isabella tried to get the ball through the goal ring. The Barton goalers had also struggled but had been just that little bit better at getting the ball through the ring.

Lily's 13-year-old brother, Steven, had watched the game. He couldn't stop laughing at Lily as she came off court with her curly hair looking wild and woolly.

'Hey look, it's Krusty the Clown!' he chortled.

Lily threw the ball at him, aiming for his head.

'He's so mean,' Maddy said sympathetically.

'Oh, I don't care. We are *so* going to get him back tonight!' she said with a wicked grin.

Even though they'd lost the game and felt a little disappointed by it, all Maddy, Prani, Sienna and Lily could think about was the sleepover they were going to have that night at Lily's house. Her home had a carpeted area in the garage, with piles of spare mattresses and even a fridge. For the first time, the four friends were allowed to sleep out there, away from the rest of Lily's family.

'We're not going to sleep at all!'

'We can go on the trampoline in the dark!'

'We can play loud music and no one will tell us to turn it down!'

'It's going to be so cool!'

That night, they ate as much junk food and drank as much soft drink as they could. They played all the songs on Sienna's iPod and danced on the trampoline for hours in the dark. Finally, Lily and her friends hatched their plan of revenge against Steven and at midnight, they put their plan into action.

'Sh,' whispered Lily, when Prani and Sienna started to laugh. 'If he hears us, he'll know.'

They crept up the side of the house in the dark, feeling their way with one hand on the wall. Sienna and Maddy each held a branch they'd pulled off the old wattle tree behind the garage.

Once in position, they all held their breath as Sienna and Maddy scraped the branches across Steven's bedroom window. Lily started making a spooky 'oooh' sound and Prani had to press her hand against her mouth in an attempt to hold in her laughter.

Sienna stubbed her toe on the side of the fence. 'Ow!'

'Shhh!'

They stumbled back down the side of the

house and fell in through the garage door, bursting with laughter.

'Oh my God!' Maddy managed to say breathlessly. 'Do you think he heard us?'

'I bet we really scared him!' Lily answered with a grin.

They collapsed onto the mattresses and crawled into their sleeping bags, but even though they were exhausted, they couldn't help reliving, over and over, the trick they had played on Steven.

It was very, *very* late when they finally got to sleep.

Chapter Seven

Maddy was completely worn out the next morning when her dad picked her up.

'Got everything?' he asked, backing the car out, carefully avoiding the large bottlebrush trees that lined the driveway. The red brush flowers hung heavily on the branches.

'Mmm, think so,' Maddy murmured, pushing her long brown hair behind her ears.

She opened her sports bag and lazily glanced inside. Then her eyes widened in alarm and she froze. Where were her netball uniform and her runners?

I thought I'd put them in my bag! So where are they? Oh, where are they? she chanted feverishly in her head. *Did I leave them at the netball clubrooms when we got changed after the game? What if they've been stolen?*

She knew her mum and dad would freak out if she'd lost her netball uniform and new runners . . . How had this happened?

'You okay?' Dad asked, glancing at her set face and her hands tightly clutching the handles of her bag.

'Oh yeah, I'm fine.' But her voice sounded fake even to her own ears, so she tried again. 'I'm just tired. Didn't get much sleep. You know how these sleepovers go!'

She tried to sound bright, but it was such a false cheeriness that Maddy was sure her dad would guess something was wrong.

Thankfully, he had tuned into the football commentary on the radio and didn't ask anything else.

The following morning, Maddy ran down the street towards school, her bag bumping against her hips in rhythm with her steps. She raced up the front steps. She was earlier than usual because she wanted to make sure she had a chance to speak to Lily before they went into class. Maddy knew she could have just called Lily yesterday to see if her things were at Lily's place – but then Mum would find out that they were missing.

Maddy stood waiting near Lily's locker, shifting from foot to foot and scanning the hallway for any sign of her friend. Finally, she spotted Lily's blonde hair in a cluster of students arriving by a side door.

'Hey Maddy!' called Lily. 'How much fun was Saturday night? Steven reckons he knew it was us at his window, but he has to be lying – why else would he have gone to sleep in the lounge room?'

Maddy interrupted Lily's cheerful chatter. 'Did I leave my netball gear at your place?'

'Huh?' Lily took a moment to adjust to Maddy's curt tone. 'Um . . . no. I know because Mum made me clean up all our mess in the garage!'

Maddy groaned and looked away.

Lily saw her friend's worried frown and the problem dawned on her. 'You've lost your netball uniform?' she asked in a stunned whisper. 'You are *so* dead. Your parents are going to kill you!'

'Maybe it's at the clubrooms,' said Maddy hopefully, as they walked to class together. Sitting in class next to Prani, working on her maths, Maddy realised that she had no choice but to sweat over it for three whole days until training on Wednesday after school, when the clubrooms would be reopened . . .

After school that day, Maddy managed once again to evade her mum's questions.

'How did your runners feel during the game? Any blisters?'

'They were fine,' Maddy answered, as briefly as she dared, setting the table with great concentration.

'You all looked great in your new netball uniforms,' her mum continued.

'Yeah.' She attempted to change the subject. 'Should I set a place for Dad? Will he be home in time?'

Maddy was relieved when her mum answered without suspicion. She didn't relax her guard, though. She knew that the moment was coming when her mum would tell her to put her uniform in the laundry for washing and, sure enough, after dinner . . .

'What do you mean, you don't have your uniform?' Mum demanded.

Maddy gulped. She was in for it now.

'I . . . ah . . . well, I . . . I think I left it in the clubrooms,' Maddy answered miserably.

'You *think*? I take it that means you don't know where you left it? Don't tell me you've lost your runners as well . . .'

Maddy nodded, looking at the tiles on the kitchen floor. She hated being in trouble.

As soon as her mum stopped questioning her, she retreated to her room and went to bed early. But she couldn't sleep; all she could do was lie there, staring at the ceiling. Where was her uniform?

Chapter Eight

By Wednesday, Maddy's optimism had returned. She had convinced herself that her netball gear was in the clubrooms and that by the end of the day, the whole miserable episode would be over.

So before training began, Maddy raced over to the clubrooms, wrenched open the door and stood in the entry, scanning the large room expectantly. She didn't immediately spot her gear but, undeterred, she began a thorough search – under the chairs, on all the tables, in every corner . . .

And nowhere could she see her netball uniform or her runners. They just weren't there. Shoulders slumped, Maddy left the clubroom and joined her teammates.

'Not there?' Sienna asked, seeing the look on Maddy's face.

Maddy shook her head.

Lily put her arm around her friend's shoulders. 'Hey, everyone!' she called out to the other girls in the team. 'Have any of you seen Maddy's netball uniform and runners?'

Most of the girls looked blankly at her and shook their heads.

'Have you seen them?' Maddy asked Phoebe, who was standing quietly to one side.

Phoebe shook her head slightly, then turned away with the same vacant expression she seemed to wear every time Maddy saw her.

Maddy didn't know what to make of Phoebe, but she didn't really think too much about it. The other girls distracted her, coming up with increasingly silly suggestions of what she could do if she still hadn't found her uniform by Saturday.

'Maybe you could share uniforms with whoever is spending time on the bench,' Sienna offered hopefully.

'Or just wear sports gear in blue and pink and hope nobody notices,' Isabella added.

'Or dazzle them with a blue and pink sari that is so spectacular the umpire will want everyone to wear the same as you!' said Prani, giggling.

And even though they all knew the rule was no uniform, no play, everyone tried to come up with some dazzling Bollywood netball moves to cheer Maddy up.

Chapter Nine

'I'm not going,' said Maddy stubbornly.

'Yes, you are,' said Mum, equally as firmly.

'But I can't play anyway!' Maddy pleaded.

'It doesn't matter. You're part of a team and you're going to support that team even if you can't play.'

Maddy frowned to hold back the tears that were threatening to fall. All she wanted to do was curl up on the couch and watch TV. It was bad enough that she couldn't play because she'd lost her uniform and runners. But now her mum wanted to humiliate her as well. She could just imagine Jade laughing when she saw Maddy turn up in her old tracksuit and worn-out runners. She *had* considered wearing something other than her sports gear but figured that'd make her stand out even more. She slumped onto her bed and looked miserably at herself in the mirror. What was the point supporting a team she would never be able to play for again, anyway? She knew her parents couldn't afford to buy her another netball uniform and another new pair of runners. Tears prickled Maddy's eyes and she rubbed them away angrily.

'Maddy, come on, please,' Mum called. 'It's time to go.'

Maddy pretended not to hear and grabbed one of the pink ribbons she and Prani had bought together, to match their Marrang uniforms. She wound it around her finger again and again.

Urghh! It just wasn't fair!

'Maddy!' called Mum.

Maddy stood up and trudged out the door after her mother. In the car, she stared out the window in a sullen silence all the way to the courts. She felt as if there was a black cloud hovering over her, which she couldn't shift.

As they pulled into the carpark, Maddy realised there were still fifteen minutes before the game started. She would have to stand with her friends before they went on to play.

She approached her teammates tentatively.

'Oh no, Maddy, haven't you got your uniform back yet?' said Lily.

Maddy just shrugged, but she felt a little better knowing that her friend cared. She stood awkwardly with some of the girls, feeling

left out, dressed in her tracksuit instead of her
netball uniform. She tied the pink ribbon in
her hair to show she belonged.

'Guess what, Maddy?' Jade exclaimed as she
came over.

'What?' Maddy's face lit up with hope.

Perhaps Jade had a spare uniform she could wear!

'I get extra time on court because you can't play today. How cool is that? I'll have one less bench shift than everyone else.'

Maddy stared at Jade. Was she really that mean or did it just not occur to her that Maddy might be upset about not being able to play?

'What?' demanded Jade, when she saw the look on Maddy's face. 'What's the problem?'

Maddy just shook her head in disgust and walked away. That was the last straw. She found a seat on the bench and plonked herself down miserably. She could see her mum and Janet talking about the game but she was too upset to go over to them. She would do the right thing today and support her team, but then she was out of here and she was *not* coming back.

Chapter Ten

Maddy felt a hand on her shoulder. She sighed deeply as she watched her team warm up. She didn't turn around.

'Yes, Mum,' she said. 'I'm supporting the team.'

'Maddy,' said a voice that wasn't her mother's.

She looked up to see Prani's mum, who was holding a plastic bag.

'I found these netball things in the bag Prani took to the sleepover. She does have a tendency to accidentally come back with more than she left with. They're not yours, are they?'

Maddy grabbed the bag without a word. She rummaged in it and saw her netball uniform and familiar-looking runners, which now looked like the best runners in the whole world.

'Oh, thank you so much!' she said. 'Mum! Mum!'

Maddy's mum looked up from where she was now talking with Sienna's mum.

'Mum, I've got my uniform!'

Maddy's mum saw the bag and, without asking any more questions, pointed towards the clubrooms and called, 'Run! Change! I'll tell Janet.'

Maddy looked towards the umpires and saw that they were checking for jewellery and long nails – the girls weren't allowed to wear any jewellery or have long nails in case they accidentally scratched another player. That meant there were only two minutes before the game started!

Maddy ducked around spectators and leapt over stray balls and bags as she raced to the clubrooms. She flung everything out of the bag as soon as she sprinted through the entrance. As quickly as she could, she pulled off her shoes, tracksuit and jumper, stuffed them into the bag, yanked the netball uniform over her head and shoved her feet into her new runners.

She raced back to the court.

Will I be in time? Will Janet put me on?

As she got closer, Maddy saw the other players walking onto the court – and for a moment she thought she had missed out. But then she saw Jade sitting on the bench with her arms crossed and a huffy look on her face – and Mum behind her, with Wing Defence bibs in her hand.

Maddy sprinted over to Mum before Janet could change her mind.

'Go for it, Maddy,' whispered Mum, as she helped Maddy attach the bibs onto her front and back. Maddy darted to her place on court just in time, because a second later, the starting whistle blew.

Maddy had to work hard to keep up with the Wing Attack from the Greenfield netball team. She was very fast and it was difficult to stop her from getting the ball. But in the second quarter, Maddy realised that even though the Wing Attack was really good at getting the ball, once she had it, she panicked and didn't know what to do with it.

So the next time she caught the ball, Maddy concentrated particularly hard on blocking her pass.

'Come forward,' the Greenfield Wing Attack entreated her teammates.

Maddy stood strong and tall in front of her, her arms held up straight, moving from side to side to block her vision.

'Here! Here!' her teammates called – but it was too late.

Brrrp, blew the whistle.

'Held ball,' announced the umpire.

Maddy took the free pass and sent the ball to Isabella, their Goal Defence, who had responded quickly to the changeover and sprinted forward into the centre third. Maddy grinned as she watched the ball make its way down the court and through to Phoebe, the Goal Shooter, who scored a goal for their team.

Maddy knew she had caused that change-over and couldn't wait to go for it again. A little while later she spotted her chance. The Greenfield Wing Attack leapt out and received the centre pass. Maddy darted in front of her, took a step back so that she was three feet away, and put her hands up to defend the pass. She could see the Wing Attack getting nervous again so she leant as far forward over the Wing Attack as she could without touching her or the ball. The Wing Attack tried to look around her for someone to pass to but Maddy held her stance until the Wing Attack began to shuffle her feet in agitation.

Brrrp!

'Stepping,' the umpire announced.

The Greenfield Wing Attack's shoulders drooped and she handed Maddy the ball for her second free throw.

Maddy turned with the ball just as Isabella streaked past her. 'Maddy, here!'

Maddy quickly threw the ball to Isabella. Isabella flicked it over the head of a tall Greenfield player straight to Lily, who was playing Centre. Lily faked a pass to Sienna in Goal Attack and instead shot the pass to Phoebe. Maddy watched as Phoebe turned and gracefully lobbed the ball up and through the goal ring. Maddy clapped and cheered. Phoebe might not say much, but it was definitely good to have her on their team as Goal Shooter!

Chapter Eleven

It was half-time and the Marrang Gems were winning by four goals. Janet was all smiles.

'Great play everyone. Let's see more of the same.' She began to reorganise the positions. 'Here you go, Maddy. Can you play Centre for the second half?'

'Yay!' Maddy took the bibs Janet offered her and gave a little jump in anticipation. She looked across to her mum and held the Centre bibs up, her eyes shining. This was the position she had wanted to try all along! Maddy loved that Centre was a running role and that you could go everywhere on the court – except, of course, for the goal circles. It meant that you were part of the play all the time.

Maddy accepted the ball from the umpire and walked out proudly to stand in the centre circle in the middle of the court. She looked around her for a moment, watching all the players take their positions and savouring the feeling of being in control.

When the whistle blew, she responded immediately. Lily was Wing Attack and she darted quickly in front of her player, so Maddy shot her a swift short pass. Lily threw the ball on to Charlotte, who was playing Goal Attack and who was free in the goal third. But as the ball sailed towards her, Charlotte closed her eyes instinctively and the ball passed right between her hands and bounced off her forehead!

Maddy gasped and stopped to see if Charlotte was okay. Charlotte's eyes were now open wide in surprise at the ball's impact but she didn't seem to be hurt and the look on her face was so comical that Maddy started laughing. Charlotte rubbed her forehead and burst out laughing too.

While everyone was distracted by Charlotte, Lily grabbed the ball, which was rolling along the ground, and passed it to Sienna, their Goal Shooter. She took aim and sent the ball hard and fast towards the ring, but it rebounded straight back into her hands – once, twice, three times!

'Bend your knees, Sienna,' Janet called from the sidelines.

So, on her fourth try, Sienna bent her knees before she released the ball, and the slight adjustment sent the ball up and through the ring.

'Woohoo! Great goal, Sienna!' Maddy called out.

Because she had taken the previous centre pass, this one would be taken by the other team's Centre. As she ran back to the centre third, she thought about where she would stand to defend Greenfield's centre pass. She decided to stand in front of the Greenfield Wing Attack. She had seen some of the older players do that so she knew it was a good way to block the Wing Attack from coming out for the pass.

Maddy spent the rest of the game running up and down the court, doing everything she could to feed the ball in to Charlotte and Sienna in the goal circle. When the whistle blew for the end of the game, Maddy came off tired. Playing Centre had been much harder than she had expected. She'd had to concentrate the whole time and run constantly.

But it had been worth the effort. It had come down to the last five minutes of the game. Greenfield had been one goal ahead so Marrang had needed two more goals to win, but somehow they had managed it.

Maddy watched Janet as she handed in her bibs, hoping that she would say something about the way she had played, but Janet only said a general congratulations to the whole team. Maddy bit her lip. She would have liked to ask Janet if she was a good Centre but she felt a bit silly asking in front of the other girls.

Just then she felt a cold, wet blast in the middle of her back. Maddy yelled in surprise and swung around to see Lily taking aim at her again, with her drink bottle. Maddy leapt across to grab her own bottle and join in the sneaky water fight that was developing. The girls alternately sipped from their bottles and took aim at anyone who wasn't looking.

'Ready to go?' Maddy's mum asked.

Maddy nodded and took pleasure in one last beautifully aimed squirt at the back of Sienna's head before darting away to join her mum at the safety of the car.

'That was a close call with your uniform,' said Mum.

'I know.' Maddy grimaced. 'I'm sorry, I'll be much more careful next time so Prani can't scoop it up with her things!'

Maddy's mum nodded. 'Great game, by the way, and a good run in Centre!'

Maddy looked up at her mum gratefully. 'Do you think so?'

'Absolutely,' her mum said with certainty.

Maddy grinned. It was good to hear her say that. She sometimes forgot that her mum used to play when she was young and knew lots about netball.

Chapter Twelve

'Okay everyone,' called Janet. 'New skill to try today: throwing a pass on the run. That means you land on one foot, step onto the other foot, then release the ball before taking another step. Sienna and Isabella, I'd like you to demonstrate – I've seen you do this before.'

Sienna and Isabella grinned at each other and ran out in front of the other girls to show them what Janet meant.

'Perfect,' Janet said, after they successfully

completed three passes. 'So, girls, what you need to do is to move from your landing foot to your other foot and then release the ball. As long as your landing foot doesn't touch the ground again while you're still holding the ball, you won't be pulled up for stepping.

'I want you all to try this with a partner, up and down one of the courts. I'll be watching to check you've got the right idea.'

Maddy grabbed a netball and ran to court two with Prani. Starting at one end, the two friends ran, flinging the ball at each other –

'Slow down, Maddy and Prani,' Janet called, moving towards them. 'Just jog slowly so that you can concentrate on your passing and steps. Okay?'

So they reined in their enthusiasm and slowed to a gentle jog. Immediately, they found it easier to count their steps and direct their passes. They moved up and down the court, feeling more and more comfortable and confident with every minute that passed.

'I think I really get this now!' said Prani.

'Me too,' said Maddy, grinning.

Maddy and Prani were so intent on the drill that they didn't notice that Janet was still watching their progress. When they reached the end of the court, Janet surprised them when she called out approvingly, 'Keep it up!'

Maddy and Prani grinned at each other and kept up their practice, but as soon as Janet stepped away to watch some of the other players, Prani couldn't help acting up. Maddy's next pass didn't make the distance and ended in a low bounce. Prani somehow managed to catch it between her knees, and she started waddling down the court.

Maddy burst out laughing. 'You look like a penguin!'

'Just smile and wave, boys. Just smile and wave,' Prani responded, with a waddle and a wave.

Maddy was laughing so hard now that she felt like she might even wet her pants! Soon, all the girls, who had come over to see what was so funny, were waddling around the court like a bunch of penguins. Even Jade joined in!

Maddy looked around her and realised they'd become a team. Learning skills together was important, but laughing together was what made them feel like they belonged. Maddy grinned as she saw even shy Phoebe try the waddle.

Janet blew her whistle and called to the group. It was a funny-sounding blow, though, because Janet was laughing too.

'Okay, okay, that's enough. We have ten minutes left – enough time for a quick practice game. Let's get moving!'

Chapter Thirteen

'Urghh . . .'

Maddy blew her nose and collapsed back against her pillow on the couch, staring listlessly at the TV.

'Here you go,' her dad announced, coming into the room. 'Doctor Dad is here with your cough medicine.'

Wrinkling her nose, Maddy sat up and sipped the spoonful of disgusting syrup.

'Urghh! That's revolting.'

Dad perched on the end of the couch and nudged Maddy's leg. 'You've been home sick from school for the last two days. I don't think you're up to playing netball tomorrow. It might be time for me to ring Janet and tell her you won't be there.'

Maddy stared at him in dismay. 'Don't call Janet! I'll be fine tomorrow. Look!' She stood up, shaking off the blanket she'd been huddling under. 'I feel heaps better. In fact, I think I'd like some fresh air. I'm going to take Boots for a walk.'

'Are you sure you're up to it?' Dad asked, with a sceptical I-know-what-you're-doing type of look.

'Yep! Couldn't be better.'

Maddy smiled brightly and walked out of the room to collect the dog lead. Desperately trying to suppress the coughing fit that threatened to bubble up out of her throat, she called to Boots, her black cocker spaniel, attached the lead to his collar, and walked outside.

As soon as she was on the footpath and out of sight, Maddy stopped and coughed heavily. Boots pulled on his lead, wondering why they were stopping before they had even started. Maddy's throat hurt and her legs felt heavy and tired. She'd only walked a few metres and already she wanted to sit down!

She gave in and perched on the low brick wall that circled the neighbour's house, her legs trembling as she hoisted herself up. Boots sat impatiently near her dangling feet.

I have to be well enough to play tomorrow, thought Maddy. *I was getting so good at running passes, and I might even get a turn in goals!*

Maddy sat on the fence for a while longer. Boots discovered her loose shoelaces and started pulling on them playfully, growling as

he tried to wrestle them out of her shoes, one at a time.

How can I get Mum and Dad to let me play? They keep telling me to drink lots of water – so that's one thing I can do. I can make sure I act hungry and eat all my dinner – that's a second thing. Okay, and third, I'll have an early night so that tomorrow I'll be full of energy for the game . . . That'll be the easiest thing to do — I want to go to bed now!

That evening, Maddy carried out her plan and her parents reluctantly agreed that she could play netball in the morning. When it was time for bed, Maddy kissed her mum and dad goodnight and went to her bedroom. Before she got into bed, she followed her usual Friday-night routine. She carefully took out her netball dress and her favourite windcheater, which was the same blue as her uniform, and hung them on the back of her bedroom door. When she climbed into bed, she lay there staring at her outfit. She couldn't wait to put it on in the morning. It was the last thing she saw as her eyes drooped shut.

Maddy woke early the next morning. Even though it was hours before the game, she dressed in her netball gear, brushed her hair and tied it into a ponytail. But as she went to tie her pink ribbon, a violent cough shook her body and she was forced to crouch over and brace herself on her knees.

I'm fine, I'm fine, she said, trying to convince herself that she was. *Once I'm on the court, I'll be so busy playing I won't even notice how I feel!*

Chapter Fourteen

Each week the girls in the team tried to make sure that they arrived at the courts with plenty of time to warm up, throw some practice passes, and shoot some practice goals. Maddy arrived and walked slowly towards her team-mates. Her legs were wobbly and she felt hot all over, even though she hadn't done anything to warm up yet.

'Maddy,' said Janet when she spotted her, 'you're in Goal Attack for the first half.'

Maddy took the bib Janet was holding out for her. Goal Attack was the most popular position. Everyone would be so jealous!

After a quick warm up, Maddy went to her position on the transverse line and eagerly waited for the umpire's whistle. But when the whistle blew, she struggled to get clear of her defender and make herself available to take the centre pass. Seeing that Jade in Wing Attack had received the ball, Maddy decided to move back into the goal third. But her legs moved as if they were made of lead, and she didn't get into position in time for Jade's pass. Shifting direction, she tried to move into the goal circle, but her body just wasn't responding and again she got there too late: she arrived just as Isabella scored her first goal as Goal Shooter. Isabella smiled happily, and everyone turned to set up for the next centre pass.

Maddy was barely able to step over the

transverse line and did nothing to try to block the other team's Wing Defence from taking the centre pass. She just stood there on the line, watching as the ball made its way to the other end of the court. She felt as if she was moving in slow motion and the rest of the team was in fast forward. After many failed attempts by the Carrington netball team to shoot a goal, Prani as Goal Keeper leapt up to catch a rebound and threw the ball into the centre third. It wasn't aimed at anyone in particular, so Maddy tried to take off after the loose ball – but she just had no energy to go after it! Her legs ached, and after two steps, she had to stop so that she could brace herself for a coughing fit. She couldn't see the ball anymore. All she could see was the ground in front of her as she bent over, coughing and coughing. Vaguely, she heard the umpire's whistle blow and she wondered what was happening. The game seemed to have stopped . . .

The next thing she knew, Janet was standing beside her.

'Maddy,' Janet said, 'you're not well. You need to come off court.'

Maddy knew Janet was right and that she couldn't go on playing. She stepped off court and allowed Janet to take off her position bibs and hand them to Charlotte. Then she slumped down onto the bench and bent over with her arms across her knees. She felt completely exhausted.

After seeing Charlotte onto the court, Janet came back over and sat beside Maddy. 'I won't be putting you back on court today, Maddy. Go home and get well.' She spoke kindly and squeezed Maddy's arm.

Maddy wasn't sure whether to be devastated or relieved but in the end, relief won. She was shivering, sweating and aching everywhere. No matter how much she wanted it, there was no way she could play netball today. What she needed was to climb into bed . . . But it was so hard to move . . .

Maddy's mum came to the rescue and helped her up off the bench.

'Come on,' she said, 'let's get you home.'

Maddy made no protest and followed her to the car. She didn't even say goodbye to the other girls, or even to Janet. As their car pulled out of the carpark, Maddy snuggled deeper into her windcheater and gave a chesty cough. For the first time since she began playing, netball wasn't the first thing on Maddy's mind. Right now, all she could think of was climbing into her cosy bed and wrapping herself in her rainbow-coloured doona.

Chapter Fifteen

Maddy's mum burst through the front door, soaking wet. 'The rain's pelting down out there!'

'I know, I only just got to the washing in time,' Maddy replied, raising her voice above the drumming of the rain on the roof, pointing to the basket by the back door.

'Thanks! That's such a help!'

'Well . . . I went out to save my netball

uniform and then figured I couldn't leave the rest out there,' Maddy admitted.

Mum laughed. 'Well, I'm still impressed. But Maddy, you do realise you won't be needing your uniform this weekend, don't you?'

'What do you mean?'

Mum bustled off to get changed into dry clothes. She called out over her shoulder, 'We're going away this weekend, remember? We've got Grandma's seventieth birthday party.'

Maddy frowned. She couldn't believe she'd forgotten Grandma's party! She'd already missed this week's training because she had still been sick, and her dismal few minutes on the court last Saturday could in no way count towards actually playing. She was starting to get really good – and now she was going to miss *another* game. She stood there absently gnawing on her lip. As much as she loved

Grandma, she really didn't want to miss the game this Saturday . . . There must be a way she could go to the game *and* the party . . .

Maddy followed her mum down the hallway.

'Mum, can't we leave for Grandma's after the game?' she suggested.

She heard her mum sigh from the bedroom. 'No, Maddy. I promised Grandma we'd get there tomorrow night so that I can start early on Saturday to help prepare the food.'

'Well, couldn't you get there tomorrow and Dad and I could get there later the next day, after the game? . . . Or maybe I could stay at Prani's for the weekend?'

Maddy knew she'd gone too far when Mum stuck her head out of the doorway, half-dressed, and used Maddy's full name.

'Madison Jane. Are you seriously telling me that you don't want to come and help and be there for your grandma on her seventieth birthday?' Her voice became increasingly shrill.

Maddy froze, embarrassed at what she'd said. 'No, Mum. I'm sorry. Of course I want to go,' she mumbled, her eyes downcast, and she retreated back down the hallway.

Maddy slumped onto the couch in the lounge room and stared out at the pouring rain. Clearly she was going to have to miss the game. Would the other girls get ahead of her?

By the time I finally get back, maybe I won't be good enough and Janet will leave me off court for the whole game! she thought, panicking. Her stomach tightened as she pictured herself sitting on the bench with Phoebe walking past, ignoring her, and Jade laughing at her from on court . . .

Her dismal thoughts were interrupted by a nudging against her hand. She looked down to see Boots gazing up at her, wagging his tail.

He always came to cheer her up when she was feeling upset. She scratched him gently behind his soft ear and, with that slightest bit of encouragement, he leapt up to lie next to her on the couch, his front paws in her lap.

Dad wandered into the room. 'Hey Maddy.'

Maddy mumbled under her breath and didn't look up.

'What's up with you, grumbles?' asked Dad.

'Oh . . . well . . . it's just . . .' Maddy frowned, looking down at Boots.

Dad sat down next to her, on the couch. 'Why do I have the feeling that this is about netball?'

Maddy started tentatively. 'It's not that I don't want to go to Grandma's, it's just that I'm missing lots of games . . .' The rest rushed out. '. . . I'm going to get behind and then I won't get as much time on court because the other girls will be so much better than me.'

'You know what?' said Dad. 'I think you might be making it harder than it needs to be. Just relax and enjoy yourself.'

Maddy looked unconvinced.

'Your mum said you're a great little netballer. She said you're even better than she was at your age, and if I know anything about sport, I know that two weeks won't make a difference. You'll be straight back into it next week, don't worry.'

Chapter Sixteen

Maddy was a little sleepy when they arrived at her grandma's house late on Friday night.

'Come inside, Possum,' Grandma welcomed her, with a big squeezy hug. 'I've got your bed all ready for you.'

Maddy melted into her grandma's arms. Grandma gave the best hugs in the whole world.

The next morning, when Maddy emerged for breakfast, the kitchen was already a hive of activity as Mum, Grandma, Aunt Kerry, Uncle Matt and Dad all prepared for the party. Maddy's younger cousins were lying in front of the TV watching a DVD, and Maddy's older cousin was sweeping the front driveway. Maddy quietly got herself a bowl of cereal.

'Aha! Maddy! There you are!' said Uncle Matt. 'Sneaking around, hoping you won't be given any chores?'

'Who, me?' said Maddy, smiling.

'Actually, come to think of it, I wished I'd done that!' added Uncle Matt under his breath. 'So what's happening with you these days? Are you playing any sport?' he asked.

'I'm a netballer,' she offered. *At least, I think I am*, she added to herself, worrying all over again that she might not be good enough now that she was missing her second game in a row.

'What? That won't do! We are a committed family of basketballers! You can't even run with the ball in netball. What sort of game is that?' he demanded with mock outrage.

'That's what makes it harder,' Maddy retorted. 'I'd like to see you try to stop in a split second when you're running at full pace.'

'Whoa, a bit of attitude,' Uncle Matt observed, 'I like it. That'll get you far in sport. A bit of push back when things get tough.'

Maddy laughed as she got up off her chair and put her bowl in the dishwasher. She knew Uncle Matt knew nothing about netball but she liked the way he teased her, as if she were one of the adults.

'So are you missing a game today, Maddy?' Aunt Kerry asked.

Maddy nodded at Aunt Kerry and then walked out of the room. She didn't want Aunt Kerry, Uncle Matt and in particular Grandma to see how disappointed she was to be missing the game.

She walked into the lounge room and had just settled down on the couch, resigned to hanging out with the little kids, when she heard the sound of a bouncing ball coming from the side of the house . . .

Chapter Seventeen

'Maddy, you're finally up!' Jack exclaimed.

Maddy's cousin Jack was a year younger than Maddy and lived miles away from her, but they always got on well when the family was together. He'd been dribbling a basketball but when he'd seen Maddy, he'd started to shuffle around the ball as he bounced, daring Maddy to try to get it. Maddy lunged in and managed to tip the ball away from him. They both chased after it and the game was on! A basketball ring was bolted to the front of the garage, so Maddy and Jack took turns dribbling the ball on approach while the other defended.

Jack quickly doubled Maddy's score.

'I'm smashing you!' he crowed.

'That's because we're playing your sport!' she countered. 'You wouldn't have a hope if we were playing netball rules.'

'Okay, bring it on!'

Maddy was pumped at Jack's willingness to try netball. She pretended that she was Janet and gave Jack a clear outline of the rules of the game.

'In netball, you're not allowed to bounce the ball to yourself, you have to pass it to someone from your team. Maybe we could use the side of the house to pass it and catch it again?'

Jack nodded.

'And you have to stand this far away from me if you're defending.' Maddy demonstrated the distance allowable.

After Maddy and Jack had agreed on the court boundaries, the game began and, for the first time ever, Maddy was getting the better of Jack. She was able to get under his defence with accurate bounce passes to the wall and quick footwork without breaking the stepping rule.

The sounds of their laughs and yells must have drifted through the house because one by one, the other cousins and the adults came to join in until, finally, Uncle Matt emerged to see what was going on.

'Noooo,' yelled Uncle Matt in mock tragedy. 'She's converted my son into a netballer!'

'It's harder than it looks, Dad,' Jack admitted.

Uncle Matt just shook his head. 'Jack, Jack, Jack,' was all he could say.

Maddy spent the rest of the day hanging out with her cousins, playing alternating games of netball and basketball. Sometimes she would help with preparations for the party but mostly she and her cousins just tried to stay out of the way of the adults as they got things ready. Occasionally her grandma would slip them something tasty to eat as the food began piling up. Finally it was time to go and get changed into her clothes for the party.

As what seemed like hundreds of unfamiliar adults streamed through the door, Maddy was grateful to have her cousins with her at the party. She helped to pass food around, feeling a little awkward as she interrupted conversations. Whenever the adults in her family were there when she approached, they would make a point of introducing her to the group. At first, Maddy wished they wouldn't – but then she realised that her grandma had already told all of her friends about her.

'This is Maddy,' Mum would say, and Maddy would smile politely.

'Oh Maddy, you're the netballer, aren't you?' one after the other would say to her.

'Oh, um . . .' Maddy hesitated the first time it happened, but the more they said it, the straighter she stood and the more confident she felt until finally, when someone asked if she was the netballer her grandma had told them about, she looked them straight in the eye and said proudly, 'Yes, that's me.'

It was a long night. When Maddy finally got into bed, tired and full of food, she nestled down into the doona. As she drifted off to sleep, she thought about how funny it was that just when she had been missing out on playing netball, people had started calling her a netballer.

Chapter Eighteen

'Prani, you'll never guess what!' Maddy said over the phone the following Monday night.

'Ooh, what?' Prani was immediately excited.

'Mum was given tickets to the Diamonds versus Silver Ferns game on Friday night and we have an extra one. Her friends got tickets and can't go for some reason. How awesome is that! Want to come?'

'Of course!' Prani giggled. 'I've just got to ask Mum.' Maddy heard Prani drop the phone and then pick it up again moments later. 'Wait, what are the tickets for again?'

Maddy laughed. She loved that Prani was so keen to come even though she didn't know what the tickets were for. 'It's a netball game between Australia and New Zealand.'

'Got it,' Prani said, then she ran off to check with her mum. In no time she was back and finalising the details with Maddy.

After hanging up the phone, Maddy stared at the tickets with the giant barcode printed across the top. So much had happened in the past few weeks – she'd lost her uniform, she'd been sick, she'd had her grandma's seventieth birthday party – that she'd forgotten about the other Madison – Madison Robinson – until her mum handed her these tickets. But now she absolutely couldn't wait to watch how Madison Robinson played to see if she could copy her game. Maybe then she could impress

Janet the next time she played, and make up for her time away.

The week seemed to drag on forever; netball was all Maddy could think about. But finally it was Friday evening and they were on their way to the game. Maddy and Prani stared through the car windows, waiting for their first glimpse of the sports arena. Streams of people were pouring out of the entrance to the carpark and walking along the wide boulevard up to the giant arena. Soon, Maddy, her mum and Prani were among them, trooping up the steps into the stadium. The talking and excitement intensified once they got inside. There were people everywhere, trying to find the right door to enter for their seats, and rushing to buy merchandise to support their team before the game began.

They passed the black and white Silver Ferns stall but didn't stop. Instead, they headed straight for the Diamonds' merchandise stand and paused, dazzled, before all the green and gold. There were sports tops, scarves, caps and key rings on display.

'So, who's your favourite player?' Prani asked Maddy, as they waited in line to buy a program.

'Madison Browne,' Maddy responded.

'Yeah right, Maddy, you wish,' said Prani.

'No, really, it's true!' Maddy insisted. 'One of the Diamonds players has the same name as me, only now she's married so her last name is Robinson.'

'Yep, she's right,' agreed the girl behind the counter.

'Really?!' Prani was impressed. 'Wow, Maddy, you'll have to get her autograph after the game.'

They turned around from the counter and began to flick through the program they'd bought, bumping into people as Maddy's mum steered them towards the entrance closest to their seats. When they emerged through the passageway, Maddy gasped at the vastness of the internal arena. Rows of seats were banked up high on each side of the court. There were two digital scoreboards and screens hanging from the massive ceiling. Camera crews and commentators were positioned courtside, and everything gleamed in the bright lights reflecting off the golden polished boards of the court. The players of both teams were already doing warm-up drills on the court.

'Prani, is Madison Robinson in the program?'

'Yeah . . . It says here that she normally plays Centre or Wing Attack and she is 168 centimetres tall,' said Prani. This didn't really help them find Madi, though, because none of the players had their bibs on yet, so Prani read on. 'Hey! She spells her name M-a-d-i, not M-a-d-d-y like you.'

Maddy screwed up her nose. 'Really?' She didn't pay much attention, though, because the players had returned to their team benches and begun to put on their position bibs. Maybe now she'd spot Madi! The commentator started to make the announcements and moments later each of the players was introduced as she ran onto the court.

'. . . And playing Wing Attack for Australia, Madi Robinson!'

Chapter Nineteen

Maddy watched as Madi Robinson ran onto the court. She looked strong and athletic. Her brown hair was in a high ponytail, just like how Maddy wore her hair when she played netball. Watching her, Maddy felt strangely proud, as if they were connected in some way.

From the first whistle of the game, Maddy was completely absorbed. She loved the way the crowd fell silent when the goalers stopped to shoot, and then roared every time their team scored a goal. Maddy was fascinated by how quickly each player ran down the court and how hard they kept working to find new positions and be ready for the ball. At times, all that could be heard was the squeak of their rubber soles on the polished boards, interspersed with the umpire's whistle, a call for the ball or the cheers of the crowd. It wasn't until after half-time that Maddy remembered that she'd vowed to watch Madi Robinson's game in particular, to see what she could learn.

The only problem was that by this time, Prani was starting to get restless. She started chatting to Maddy about when she thought the next sleepover might be, if her mum would let her have it at their house or if maybe Maddy would have it at hers . . .

Maddy knew that Prani really only played netball just to be with her friends, that she wasn't as fired-up about netball as Maddy was.

But even though Maddy knew that Prani was getting bored, she still didn't really want to talk – she wanted to watch Madi Robinson play.

'Hey Prani, did you see that intercept?' Maddy asked, trying to get Prani interested in the game.

But Prani just kept chatting – and now she couldn't even sit still. First she began squirming in her seat, then she stood up to look behind her, which made her seat spring up with a bang. When she plonked back down, she made all of the seats in the whole row shake – and Maddy could tell from the looks people were giving her that Prani was starting to annoy the people around them.

Maddy spotted her mum making her way back along the row with a bucket of popcorn.

'Yay! Popcorn!' Prani chirped, and for the next little while she sat still in her seat, munching happily.

'Thanks, Mum,' Maddy said, giving her a warm smile. Her mum always knew how to make things work.

Maddy grabbed a handful of popcorn and turned her attention back to the game.

What does Madi do that makes her so good?

The more Maddy watched, the more she realised that Madi pushed hard for everything. She never waited for the ball, she grabbed it. She never called from behind; she always got in front of her player.

I can do that, Maddy thought to herself. *Maybe if I do that in the next game, Janet will notice. She keeps telling us to get in front . . .*

After watching Madi Robinson for the rest of the third quarter, Maddy felt confident that she had some useful tips. In the final quarter of the game, she turned her attention to enjoying Prani's company and barely watched the game. They took turns flicking popcorn at different targets, mostly the clumps of Silver Ferns supporters, until Maddy's mum caught them out and removed the popcorn bucket. Then they tried to start a Mexican wave going through the crowd, with no success at all.

When the final siren went, Maddy started cheering for the Diamonds' win but Prani grabbed her wrist. 'Come on. Let's go down to the barrier. We have to get Madi's signature!'

The two of them raced down to get a good position at the barrier above the Diamonds' team bench. They hung over the rail, waving their program and pen to get the players' attention. The Diamonds did their warm-down laps on the court and then wandered back to the bench for a drink. Finally, a few of the players came over to the waiting fans.

'Madi! Madi!' Maddy called, but she didn't look over.

'MADI! THIS GIRL HAS THE SAME NAME AS YOU!' Prani bellowed, loud enough for the whole stadium to hear. She started giggling madly as she pointed at Maddy with both hands.

Maddy went bright red but it worked: Madi Robinson walked over.

'Hey, is that true?' she said.

'Uh-huh,' said Maddy, nodding timidly and handing Madi the program to be signed. 'My name's Maddy Browne.'

'Well, you might have to take my place when I get too old to play,' Madi said, grinning.

'What did she write?' Prani asked, after Madi had moved on to speak to other fans.

Maddy held out the program. 'To my replacement, best wishes, Madi Browne-Robinson.'

Maddy hugged it to her chest and headed back up the stairs to where her mum was

waiting. She knew exactly the spot on her bedroom wall where this was going.

After they had dropped Prani off home, Maddy and her mum headed inside to get ready for bed. Maddy saw the answering machine on the hall table. 'Oh Mum, look – there's a phone message.' She pressed the flashing light and Janet's voice came through clearly.

'Hi, this is Janet speaking. I just wanted to make sure that Maddy will be back for the game tomorrow. We're playing an experienced team and we'll need her.'

'Well,' said Mum, with her eyebrows raised, 'it looks like you're a valued player, Miss Browne.'

Maddy raised her eyebrows back at her mum and put on a silly glamour pose with one hand in the air and the other on her hip. But even though she was making a joke of it, secretly she was thrilled that Janet would call to make sure that she was playing tomorrow. Maybe she wasn't going to be left on the bench after all!

Before she climbed into bed, Maddy prepared all of her netball gear ready for the morning, including her ribbon and shoes and socks. She also found some Blu-Tack and stuck the program with Madi's autograph to the display wall in her bedroom. She pictured Madi pushing forward, always forward, for the ball, and constantly working to catch the next pass.

As Maddy lay in bed, her muscles were restless, ready for action. She felt like she could run out onto the court right now and play just as well as the other Madison.

Chapter Twenty

At the courts the next day, Maddy couldn't contain her impatience to know what position she was going to play. More than anything, she wanted to play Wing Attack, the same position that Madi had played last night. She knew that it irritated Janet when the players nagged her about different positions but she just couldn't wait any longer to find out.

'Um, Janet, where did you want me to play today? I just wanted to . . . um . . . to be able to . . . ah . . . prepare,' she stammered when Janet turned and looked at her.

'Wing Attack,' said Janet firmly, then she looked away again, making it clear that there wasn't to be any argument.

But there was no way Maddy was arguing with that! She skipped over to Prani in delight and gave her a high five.

'Yes! Wing Attack!' Then she added in a confidential whisper, 'I can try the new moves we saw Madi do last night.'

'Go Maddy! Go Maddy!' Prani chanted. 'Hey, can I have your autograph?'

'Sh,' Maddy said, laughing, as they walked over to the team bag and grabbed a ball to do some warm-up passes.

When it was time for the game to start, Maddy moved into position on court. She watched Sienna step into the centre circle holding the ball, ready for the whistle.

Maddy felt tense but with a clear sense of what she wanted to do this game.

Go forward, she kept repeating to herself. But the girl next to her from the Central Park team was sticking so closely that it was going to be almost impossible for her to get in front. As Maddy saw the umpire raise the starting whistle to her mouth, she leapt forward – but she was a fraction ahead of the sound.

Brrp! it went.

'Breaking,' the umpire announced, giving the ball to the Central Park Wing Defence. Maddy winced. She had just lost her team the ball. She couldn't waste it like that! Sure of her disapproval, Maddy didn't dare risk a look at Janet. Instead, she pushed what had happened out of her mind and focused on the game, looking for her next chance.

Before long, Prani as Goal Defence caught a rebound after the Central Park Goal Attack tried for a goal. She sent the ball back down the court. Maddy bounced lightly on the balls of her feet so she'd be ready for a pass. When Lily in Wing Defence turned with the ball, Maddy sprinted forward away from her player. Lily saw that Maddy was free and sent the ball flying towards her. Maddy's opponent caught up to her and reached out, but Maddy pushed forward and grabbed the ball out of the air.

Mine, she thought to herself with satisfaction.

Maddy looked for someone to throw to. Jade in Goal Attack and Sienna in Centre were both calling for the ball – but they were both behind their players.

Maddy shook her head. *Not a safe pass.*

'Maddy!' she heard Lily call from behind her. Maddy turned and off-loaded the pass. She could hear Janet's voice in her head:

'Sometimes you have to pass back to move forward.'

Lily sent the ball through to Jade, who had darted to the side.

Go forward, Maddy thought to herself, and so she raced towards Jade, calling for the pass. She was so proud of herself for breaking free from her player that she didn't realise that she had got too close! Jade could hand her the ball from here rather than throw it, and the umpire would call that a short pass, which was not allowed. Jade frowned in frustration. She looked around and threw a desperate wonky lob in the general direction of Phoebe as Goal Shooter instead. Phoebe somehow managed to pluck it out of the air and put it through for a goal.

'Phew,' Maddy said, exhaling loudly in relief. *That was close! This is harder than it looked last night!*

The next time a Central Park player had the ball, Maddy deliberately hung back a little to leave room to run forward in case her team got an intercept. When Prani tapped a rebound to Isabella as Goal Keeper, Maddy was ready, running forward to call for the ball. After throwing the ball on to Jade, Maddy sprinted down to the goal third. She let her player follow her down the court, then quickly changed direction and ran towards Jade.

'Jade! Over here!' she called.

This time she wasn't too close. Jade passed the ball smoothly to Maddy, who slipped it to Sienna, who fed the ball in to Phoebe.

Now I'm getting the hang of it, said Maddy to herself. She felt the adrenalin buzzing through her legs and allowed herself a glance to the sidelines where she saw her mum smiling and Janet clapping.

'No breaking! Get in front!' Janet urged the Gems.

Maddy stood behind the line, ready for the whistle. She was determined not to break this time – but she was equally determined not to let her player get in front of her. Just as the umpire raised the whistle, Maddy bent her knees in readiness. The whistle went and Maddy leapt in front of the Central Park Wing Defence. Sienna grinned and sent Maddy a quick chest pass, and Maddy had the ball sailing overhead to Jade before the Central Park players even knew what was happening. Moments later, they had another goal.

'Yay! Woohoo!' The Marrang Gems hooted in pleasure as they continued to get the better of the feared Central Park team.

Chapter Twenty-one

'Great play, everyone. Remember: short, safe passes are always the way to go. And safe is what we need if we want to keep winning this game.' It was half-time and Janet had brought the team all in together. 'Has anyone noticed how Maddy is getting in front of her player and coming forward for the pass? That's what I want all of you to do.'

Maddy bit into her orange quarter to hide her proud grin. She had dreamed of this happening but never really believed it would come true. She had tried out some of Madi's moves and they had actually worked! She took a deep breath to try to settle her jittery stomach but this time it wasn't anxious jitters, it was happy jitters.

It doesn't get better than this! Maddy thought to herself.

Spurred on by their success in the first half of the game, the girls continued to outplay Central Park. Maddy's efforts were rewarded with a whole game in Wing Attack, and with everyone working to get in front of their players, the Gems played better than they ever had before.

Brrp, went the umpire's whistle, calling for the end of the game.

They had won!

The girls jumped into the air, cheering.

'That was the best game ever! Go Gems!' yelled Maddy, her eyes shining.

'It was awesome!' agreed Lily.

The girls all tried for a joint high five. They leapt up into the air – only to fall on top of each other, laughing, as half of them mistimed their jumps and missed each other's outstretched hands.

It took a while but finally Maddy's mum managed to drag her away to head home.

'Great game, Maddy, you played so well!' Mum said. 'So should we sign you up for another sport next season now that you've tried netball? You're probably getting a bit sick of it now, aren't you?' she teased.

'Mum,' Maddy said in mock huffiness, 'I will have you know that I am now officially hooked on netball so there will be no changing sports!'

Maddy caught her reflection in the glass of the clubroom door as they walked past. She grinned to herself.

That's right – I'm a netballer!

Player Profile

Maddy Browne

Full name: Madison Jane Browne
Nicknames: Maddy, Mads
Age: 12
Height: 146 centimetres
Family: Mum and Dad
School: Marrang Public
Hobbies: Maddy has enjoyed playing netball
for more than half her life! She first started

netball when she was five years old when her Mum enrolled her in NetSetGO training. This is where she learnt the basic rules of netball. After school and on the weekends, Maddy loves watching professional netball matches and learning new moves. She is so hooked on netball that every Friday night she sets out her Gems uniform and tries to guess what position she will get to play in the game the next day. Maddy likes keeping fit by taking her black cocker spaniel, Boots, to the park and by playing basketball with her cousin, Jack. She also enjoys having sleepovers with her Gems teammates, especially with her best friend, Prani. Maddy hopes that the next sleepover can be at her house.

Netball club: Marrang Netball Club

Netball team: Marrang Gems, the Marrang Netball Club Under 13s team

Netball coach: Janet

Training day: Wednesday

Netball uniform: Royal blue netball dress with white side panels where 'Marrang' is written in pink. Maddy also likes to wear a pink ribbon in her hair to match the pink on her uniform.

Favourite netball positions: Wing Attack, Centre

Netball idol: Australian Diamonds and Melbourne Vixens player Madison Robinson

Best netball moment: Playing Wing Attack for the Marrang Gems and being pivotal in their win against Central Park and putting into practice some of the moves she learnt from watching Madi Robinson.

Netball ambition: To one day play for the Diamonds. In the meantime, her goal is to win every centre pass for her team.

Netball Drills

Perfect Passing Practice

1. Grab a partner and a netball.
2. Stand about three metres apart and face your partner.
3. Practise 20 throws of each of the passes described below.

Shoulder Pass

Hold the ball in one hand. Bend your elbow so that the ball is sitting in your hand and your hand is around the same level as your shoulder. Throw the ball using only that hand.

Chest Pass

Hold the ball in both hands and push it out from chest height.

Lob Pass

Use one hand to throw the ball high so that it makes an arc in the air before it reaches your partner. Try to throw it high enough so that your partner needs to jump to catch the ball.

Bounce Pass

Hold the ball in both hands. Bounce the ball on the ground between you and your partner so that it bounces up into the hands of your partner.

HOT TIP

Try swapping partners to mix up the challenge.

How to Be Amazing in the Goal Circle: Lead, Receive and Shoot

1. GS and GK start in the goal circle.
2. All other players stand around the goal circle.
3. GS starts with the ball. GS has to pass the ball out to one of the players around the goal circle three times before being allowed to shoot.
4. Each time the GS passes the ball to one of the players around the goal circle, the GS tries to get into a better position to shoot for goal.
5. GK defends and tries to intercept the passes.
6. Players on the outside of the goal circle need to use accurate lob, bounce and chest passes to prevent the ball from being intercepted

by the GK, and to help GS get into a better position for shooting goals.

HOT TIP
Try practising with a GS and GK that are different heights.

Be the Fastest and Pass on the Run

1. Grab a partner and a netball.
2. Stand three metres apart, both facing the same direction.
3. Move together in a slow jog down the court.
4. Pass the ball between you as you go.
5. When you catch the ball and land on one foot, take one step with the other foot and then pass the ball to your partner.
6. Remember: the first foot that hits the ground after you catch the ball is your landing foot. As long as your landing foot doesn't touch the ground again when you are holding the ball, you won't be pulled up for stepping.

HOT TIP
Try speeding up as you get better at your footwork.

NETBALL GEMS

Chase Your Goal

Written by **B. HELLARD** and **L. GIBBS**
Illustrated by **CAT MACINNES**

RANDOM HOUSE AUSTRALIA

Chapter One

Phoebe stretched up to reach an impossibly high pass. She caught it expertly and then, under pressure from the defenders, passed it on quickly. Dodging around the opposing team's Goal Defence, she raced towards the goals to catch the next pass . . . But the pass came back to her before she was ready.

Nooo!

Somehow Phoebe managed to catch it . . . But she was off balance.

Oh no! I'm going to fall!

Phoebe teetered just inside the back line of the goal circle, her heart hammering wildly in her chest. But hearing the crowd yelling encouragement strengthened her resolve and she concentrated on bending her knees to centre herself.

I can do this!

Smoothly, Phoebe turned and raised the ball above her head. The goal ring was right above her. The crowd fell silent. All eyes were on her. The Goal Defence was straining to block her view but her arms barely registered in Phoebe's vision. She pictured in her mind the ball curving over the defender's hand and through the ring. A sense of calm descended over her. She gracefully sent the ball on its arc and it sailed through the ring for another goal. The crowd went wild, yelling and stomping their feet.

With a thrill of excitement, Phoebe allowed herself a little wave to her fans before turning back to the game.

'Phoebe! Dinner's ready!' Mum called from the back door.

Phoebe dropped her arm in embarrassment. 'Okay, I'll be there in a minute, Mum.' She looked around as the crowd melted away. *One last goal before I go in.*

She grabbed the ball and bounced it off the brick wall at the side of her house. It ricocheted back, but she allowed it to bounce first on the concrete before catching it. She took one step forward and aimed for the free-standing goal ring Dad had set up for her in the backyard. The ball went up . . . up . . . and straight through for another goal.

Phoebe spent hours out here whenever she could. Her dad had created this training area for her when she'd first started NetSetGO training as a little girl and she'd been learning the basic skills and rules of netball. Practising netball was her favourite thing to do when she was at home. She loved pretending she was playing for Australia and that the crowd was cheering for her. In her fantasy, she was relaxed and confident, and everyone thought she was awesome.

Phoebe screwed up her nose. Her real life was very different to her fantasy life. *As if I could be like that in front of a crowd. I don't even feel comfortable talking to the girls in my own team!*

Her team, the Marrang Netball Club Under 13s – or the Marrang Gems, as they had named themselves – were improving their game every week, but . . .

I wish I could just relax and act normal around them!

'Phoebe!' Mum called again, sounding slightly annoyed this time.

Phoebe dropped the ball and hurried inside for dinner. Her skin was flushed and her long light-brown hair hung in a sleek plait. She could hear her dad talking in his booming voice as she approached the kitchen. Dad and Phoebe's brother Max were discussing soccer tactics, while Mum was preparing to serve up dinner. Phoebe frowned as the smell of the sarma reached her. Phoebe's mum loved to cook the traditional Croatian meal of cabbage, minced meat and rice, which she had learnt to make from her mother, but Phoebe thought it smelt horrible when it was cooking.

Phoebe slid into her seat and watched as her dad jumped out of his to demonstrate a move to Max. Dad was square and solid, but surprisingly agile.

'And then if you do this – you should be able to steal it from him.'

Dad danced around an imaginary ball, shooting his leg out at the last minute. But his foot caught the edge of his chair and he staggered across the kitchen floor, narrowly missing the hot dish Phoebe's mum was carrying to the table.

'Yeah, thanks, Dad,' Max smirked. 'I'll definitely try losing my balance and stumbling around!'

Chapter Two

Once they were all settled at the table, Phoebe's dad turned his attention to her.

'So how did training go tonight?' he asked.

'I didn't have training tonight,' Phoebe replied, confused.

'No, I meant your own training, out the back,' Dad explained.

'Oh, yeah,' Phoebe murmured. 'It was fun.' She looked down at her plate, blushing a little, hoping he hadn't seen her waving to the imaginary crowd.

'What's that?' said Dad. 'I can't hear you!'

Phoebe felt her face go even redder.

Mum put her hand on Dad's arm. She studied Phoebe for a moment. 'We all know that quiet murmur is your shy voice,' she said gently, 'but you'll need to be a bit louder. I noticed that during the warm-up at your netball game on Saturday you were talking very quietly as well. It would be a shame if the girls thought you were ignoring them. You don't want them to get the wrong idea, do you?'

'No, Mum,' said Phoebe, sighing.

Mum was right. She *had* felt extra shy at netball.

Had the girls taken me the wrong way? Phoebe thought. *Did they really think I had been rude? Is that why I haven't made friends with them as quickly as Lily and Sienna have?*

Maybe that's why Jade always looks at me as if I were an alien . . .

'How many out of ten?' asked Dad, breaking into her thoughts.

'Sorry, what, Dad?' Phoebe welcomed the change of topic but she wasn't sure what he was asking.

'Your goaling – how many can you get in out of ten?'

'I'm not sure. I wasn't counting.'

'It's really important you keep practising until you can get ten out of ten,' he said. 'Then the coach will pick you for goals every time! Why don't we go back out after dinner and see where you're at.'

Phoebe's eyes lit up. *More goaling practice before bed – cool!*

Phoebe quickly finished her dinner and headed back outside. Dad soon followed and they started with some regular goaling practice from directly in front of the goals. Dad commentated constantly as Phoebe goaled, encouraging her and admiring her technique. Still primed from her session before dinner, Phoebe managed to get nine shots in a row before one bounced back off the ring.

'Awesome work,' said Dad, passing the ball back to Phoebe. 'Now let's mix things up!'

He started Phoebe right in front of the goal ring, where she had been standing before. But this time, with each goal that went through, she had to take a step backwards, to increase the challenge, and for each one she missed she was allowed to take a step forward, to make it a little easier. Phoebe loved the new drill. She concentrated on increasing the bend in her knees to get the extra push needed for the ball to make the distance. Before long, Phoebe was shooting from beyond the distance of a standard goal circle and Dad suggested that she include sideways steps to change the angle she had to shoot at, and to increase the challenge even more. Phoebe was completely absorbed in the drill and quickly learnt to master that, too.

'You're a star!' he said. 'Where did you learn to goal so well?'

'Caitlyn,' she said. Caitlyn looked after Phoebe and Max when their parents went out. She was an amazing netballer and often came out to the backyard with Phoebe, patiently teaching her everything she knew about netball.

'Excellent. Now, let's see how you do under pressure.'

This time they repeated the drill, but Dad defended every shot. He danced around in front of her, waving his arms and pulling faces to distract her. Phoebe tried to focus on goaling but her dad looked so ridiculous that she soon started giggling.

'Dad! You can't dance around on court!'

'Doesn't matter,' he puffed. 'Just goal!'

Phoebe grinned and went back to goaling. It was hard pretending she was playing for Australia with her dad's moustache twitching every time he stretched to defend, but it was lots of fun training with him!

Chapter Three

Thick fog enveloped Phoebe on her walk to the school bus stop. Traffic sounds were muffled, the trees were still and she could barely see five metres in front of her. All was calm. Even the birds were silent. The familiar street had become a mysterious world, with shadowy shapes emerging and disappearing as she walked along. Phoebe loved it. It was like being invisible! All too often she had people bothering her, wanting to talk to her . . .

'Phoebe! Can we have a minute?'

Oh no! Not reporters again!

A chubby man emerged from the fog, hefting a camera onto his shoulder. The tall blonde woman with him thrust a large black microphone forward. Phoebe plastered a cheery smile onto her face.

'How have you managed with all the publicity lately?' said the woman. 'I mean, everyone knows who you are, especially after the camera followed you to last week's game and filmed that amazing goal you scored. The viewers love you!'

Phoebe glanced at the camera, noting the red light blinking to show it was filming. 'Oh, it's fine!' she said, casually. 'I just go about my business and pretend that no one's watching.'

'Well, we know that!' the reporter replied. 'After all, it *is* a reality show!'

Phoebe grinned, tossing her plait behind her shoulder. 'You sort of forget that the cameras are there after a while. I'm just being me!'

The reporter fired another question. 'Just between us . . .' She leant closer to Phoebe, as if sharing a secret. 'How did you get chosen to be on *Real Schoolgirls of Marrang*?'

'I was spotted in a supermarket. It was Saturday morning so I was in my netball uniform, and I was buying breakfast cereal and singing.' Phoebe laughed. 'Sometimes I just do things like that. I don't care what people think of me, I just am who I am!'

The reporter turned to the camera. 'Well, you heard it here first! Only Phoebe would have the confidence to sing in the supermarket!'

With a parting wave, Phoebe flashed a final smile at the camera. 'Make sure you watch me next week!'

Suddenly, two headlights appeared out of the fog, growing larger and clearer. As the bus pulled up to the curb, the reporters and cameras Phoebe had imagined faded away.

Turning back to reality, Phoebe climbed the steps onto the bus, banging her backpack on the door in the narrow entry. Making her way to an empty seat, she tripped on a boy's computer bag and staggered awkwardly down the aisle. The boy and his mate sniggered and the students packed into the bus all turned to stare at her.

Blushing, Phoebe slid quietly into her seat.

Chapter Four

'White line runs. Go!'

Eight girls took off. They jogged to the first white line that divided the court into three, then returned to the end of the court. Turning around, they jogged a little faster to the second white line, and again returned to the end. On the final run, they sprinted to the very end of the court, their legs flashing and their arms pumping.

'Again!'

There were eight dramatic groans, but everyone moved off in a group to repeat the drill.

Netball training for the Marrang Gems always began with some kind of warm-up. Often it was a set of simple exercises but today was particularly chilly, and Phoebe was glad that they were running.

Phoebe jogged next to Maddy and Prani. She could hear them giggling together at Prani's silly running style – she looked like a waddling duck. Phoebe wished she had a close friend in the team, someone to laugh with, the way Prani and Maddy did. She knew Charlotte pretty well but they weren't close friends or anything; they just went to the same school. She really liked Lily, though. It was Lily's mum, Janet, who was their coach. Lily was always nice to her, but Phoebe just didn't know what to do to become her friend.

After their warm-up, the girls paired off automatically, grabbing netballs for passing practice. Although this was the predictable part of each training session, and Phoebe always partnered with Charlotte, Charlotte's passes were anything but predictable! Sometimes the ball came straight to Phoebe, but other times it would go much too high or wildly off course.

'Oops! Sorry!' Charlotte apologised for the tenth time.

But Phoebe didn't mind trying to catch balls coming towards her from all over the place. It was never boring!

On the other side of the court, Phoebe heard Janet's voice.

'Sienna, you know your hair should be up. You can't practise with it blowing in your face. Go and get a hair tie out of my sports bag.'

A few moments later, Sienna sprang up from where she had been crouching near Janet's bag and walked back onto the court. 'I'm ready now,' she announced dramatically.

Each of the girls looked over at Sienna. She had one hand on her hip and she strode across the court as if she were a model on a catwalk.

The girls abandoned their passing drills and started laughing hysterically.

Sienna stopped in a theatrical pose. 'What?' she asked, innocently.

This made the other girls laugh even harder – because Sienna had used about seven hair ties to gather her hair into as many clumps, all over her head! A particularly thick clump draped down over her forehead and covered her eyes.

'I can't see very well,' Sienna added. 'Is something wrong?'

Phoebe saw that even Janet, who was busy setting up for the next drill, couldn't help but grin – Sienna just looked so funny.

Phoebe laughed along with the other girls but quickly forgot about Sienna's hair when she spotted the cones and ladders Janet was arranging on the court. There were two sets of cones running alongside each other in parallel lines, and two long, flexible ladders on the ground beside the cones.

I wonder what we have to do with those, thought Phoebe.

She looked over to the rest of her teammates to see if they were wondering the same thing. But they were now pulling out their own hair ties and rearranging their hair so that pony-tails sprang from the sides of their heads, or flopped over their faces.

Janet pressed on with the training, ignoring the girls' antics.

'Today is all about footwork and balance,' she announced. 'The cones and ladders are going to help with that. You will need to change the way you move to get around the obstacles, while keeping your body balanced. Watch my footwork as I go around the stations.'

Janet stood at the top of the ladder but side-on, so that the ladder stretched out to her right. She moved sideways along the ladder, dancing lightly on her toes, in a quick high-stepping movement between each rung.

'When you have done this several times, I'll be challenging you to look ahead, instead of down at your feet.'

Next Janet stood facing a line of cones so that the cones stretched out in front of her.

Lily moved closer to Phoebe so that she could also see what Janet was demonstrating.

'For this drill,' continued Janet, 'you need to run from the first cone to the last one. The hard part is that to get there, you will have to dodge around each cone, like this . . .' Janet took off, darting around the cones, planting her outside foot on the ground next to each one to help anchor her body and keep perfectly balanced. 'Did you watch my feet?'

Phoebe and Lily nodded, but the rest of the girls were still fiddling with their hair or laughing behind their hands at each other's crazy hairdos.

'Well then,' said Janet, 'hop into a line and let's see how you go.'

Phoebe hung back. She watched the rest of her teammates push each other forward to go first and, when they got to the front of the line, burst haphazardly into action.

It was obvious as soon as they started that they had barely listened to the instructions. Some of the girls landed awkwardly on the plastic rungs of the ladder, or wove in a curvy movement around the cones. Phoebe was sure that a few of them couldn't even see through their forward-hanging ponytails.

Most of them collapsed into giggles when they tripped.

Phoebe giggled along with the others, but she didn't feel confident enough to join in on the fun. Instead, she quietly waited for her turn and then, head down, watching where her feet needed to go, she began. It felt weird at first, to dance sideways in tiny steps. But by the time she got to the second ladder, it felt a little less awkward. The cones were a different matter. She couldn't remember how Janet's footwork had looked, so her first attempt was unbalanced and she even nudged one of the cones with her foot.

The coach's whistle blew as she turned to face the team. 'Well, that was a disaster,' she said, raising her eyebrows and looking sternly at those with the craziest hairdos. 'This time, if you make three mistakes, you'll be doing three laps of the court!'

At the threat of running laps, the girls hastily rearranged their hair so that they could see properly, and they gave their full attention when Janet demonstrated the exercise one more time.

When they tried the ladders and cones again, there was a huge improvement. On their third or fourth try, the girls were smiling in triumph as they stepped neatly between the ladder rungs and dodged around the cones. Some of them even managed to lift their eyes occasionally rather than staring intently at their feet.

'Now I'm seeing some balance!' said Janet, smiling in approval.

Chapter Five

For the last part of training, the Marrang Gems were to practise their footwork and balance in a pretend netball set-up. Janet placed each of the eight girls around the goal circle. She held only one netball.

'All of you are playing the positions of Centre and Wing Attack. As you know, when you play in these positions, you need to focus on helping your goalers. This means that when the ball is inside the goal circle, you need to stand by, ready to take a pass, in case one of the goalers needs to pass the ball out of the goal circle to get into a better position to shoot.

'Phoebe and Isabella, can you come over here? Okay. Phoebe, you're Goal Shooter and Isabella, you're Goal Keeper.'

Everyone waited expectantly, their eyes fixed on Janet.

'Phoebe will start with the ball. She has to pass the ball out of the goal circle – to any of you Wing Attacks and Centres – three times before she is allowed to shoot. Each time Phoebe passes the ball out, she will try to get into a better position to shoot for a goal. She will need to use fast footwork and focus on her balance so that she can dodge away from Isabella while she tries to get into a better position to shoot.'

All the girls nodded to show they understood what they were meant to do.

'Isabella, your job is to try to defend Phoebe. You might even manage to intercept the ball. You will need to use fast footwork and focus on your balance, as well, so that you can keep track of Phoebe everywhere she goes.

'Does anyone have any questions about how the drill works? No? Okay, great. Play!'

Phoebe passed the ball before Isabella even had time to focus. Maddy took the pass, grabbing the ball firmly, and then snapped the ball straight back to Phoebe, who had darted across the goal circle. Phoebe threw the ball back to Jade but found Isabella defending tightly against her. She dropped back and called for a lob from Jade. The high ball sailed to Phoebe, out of Isabella's reach. Phoebe took it and swung around immediately, passing the ball to Lily who was standing on the opposite side of the circle. Isabella raced over just in time to block a return pass, so Lily sent a neat bounce pass under Isabella's arm to Phoebe, who was standing by the baseline. In a matter of only seconds, Phoebe had made her three passes and had positioned herself perfectly so that she was ready to shoot! This was one drill that felt completely natural to her. It was almost exactly how she practised in her backyard! For the first time at netball training, she felt truly confident.

'Great work, Phoebe!' called Janet. 'I can see you've been practising a lot.'

Phoebe murmured her thanks shyly, looking down at the ground, but inside she was glowing.

When training finished, Phoebe walked over to where she'd put her drink bottle, at the edge of the court. Lily appeared beside her.

'You were awesome, Phoebe! I can't believe how good you were at that drill. Mum nearly swallowed her whistle!'

Phoebe smiled. What could she say back to Lily? She picked up her drink bottle, trying to think of something interesting to say and getting more and more anxious by the second that Lily would give up trying to talk to her and walk away.

'So tell me your secret,' Lily chatted on.

'Um . . .' Phoebe looked away. 'Well, I do a lot of passing and shooting practice at home.' Her voice was so quiet she could barely hear it herself.

Lily stopped walking and looked at her expectantly. 'What? I can't hear you. YOU'LL HAVE TO SPEAK LOUDER!' She grinned and gave Phoebe a nudge.

Lily's friendly teasing made Phoebe feel more relaxed, so that this time she spoke loudly. 'I do a lot of passing and shooting practice at home.'

'Do you have a goal ring in the backyard?' asked Lily.

'Yeah . . . And I also have a mini goal circle painted on the concrete, and it's set up close to the back of the house so I can throw the ball against the wall instead of someone passing it to me . . .'

'No way!' said Lily. 'That's seriously cool!'

Phoebe gave Lily a small smile. She thought so, too. In fact, everything about today was seriously cool. She had completed the drills really well, Janet had liked how she'd played, and finally she'd spoken to Lily!

Chapter Six

Lily and Phoebe reached the other girls gathered around their water bottles and sports bags. Lily stretched over Isabella to grab her bag. As she pulled it towards her, a square white envelope fell out.

'Hey, what's this?'

All the girls gathered around.

Lily opened the envelope and read what was inside. Her eyes widened in surprise.

'What does it say?' asked Maddy.

'It's a riddle, with a . . . sort of . . . puzzle piece . . . I think. It's really weird.'

'Let me see! Yeah, pass it around!' the girls called out.

But before Lily could show anyone, Sienna said, 'Lily, I got one too! But mine came in the mail!'

'I can't believe you didn't say something earlier!' said Lily.

'Well, I got here a bit late, so I didn't have a chance to,' said Sienna.

'Did you bring yours?' asked Lily.

The rest of the girls were turning their heads from Lily to Sienna, as if they were watching a tennis match. No one had any idea what they were talking about! Sienna rummaged around in her bag, fished out her white envelope, and pulled out two pieces of paper – one a large rectangle, the other a small square. They looked identical to Lily's pieces of paper.

'So? What do they say?' demanded Jade.

The two girls began reading aloud from their large rectangular piece of paper, each with a cluster of girls peering over their shoulders.

'Here is a puzzle to be solved by you,
when you are all down at the court.

Look out for a clue, or maybe two;
don't rush, give it plenty of thought!'

Lily and Sienna looked up at each other. Everyone started speaking at once.

'What does it mean?' asked Prani.

'Who is it from?' wondered Isabella.

'It mentions the netball courts. Do you think it's from Janet?' asked Charlotte.

'Nah, it's not Mum,' said Lily. 'But I reckon it's got something to do with all of us – because it talks about all of us!'

Sienna nodded. 'Yeah, and it says there are going to be more clues coming!'

'Ooh, a mystery!' said Maddy, in an awed whisper. 'My dad loves mystery shows. Maybe it's a ransom note!'

'Seriously, Maddy?' Jade scoffed. 'No one has gone missing.'

Lily decided to get everyone back on track. 'You've forgotten about the second piece of paper we got! Move over so Sienna and I can compare our weird little squares.'

Lily nudged Prani off the seat and placed her square down where everyone could see it. There were three things written on it:

```
You
birth
Sunda
```

Sienna put her square on the seat next to Lily's.

```
a
on
2.00 pm
```

All eyes stared down at the two squares of paper. At last Charlotte ventured a question. 'Um . . . Was one of you born on a Sunday? . . . At two o'clock?'

'Don't know,' Lily muttered, staring at the two squares. 'Weird . . . Really weird.'

'Maybe it's one of those creepy chain letters that say something terrible is going to happen to you if you don't forward it to five friends,' Jade suggested.

A sea of horrified faces stared back at her.

'No, it wouldn't be that,' Sienna assured everyone.

'Maybe it's about someone's birth*day*,' Lily offered.

She picked up her square of the puzzle to have a closer look, and as she did, Charlotte squeaked. 'There's something on the back. Look!'

Lily turned her square over and saw that there was a coloured splotch covering the back.

Sienna snatched up her square and turned it over. There was colour on the back of her square as well!

'I can't tell what it is,' said Sienna.

Once again, everyone stared at the squares, trying desperately to see a picture in the blurred colours.

'Well, whatever it's about,' Lily said, 'we've got a few days, at least, to think about it and see what we can come up with. That's what the rhyme said – we have to solve it at the courts, and we're here on Wednesdays for training and Saturdays for the game.' She looked around the circle, a mischievous grin on her face. 'So be ready for anything. Woooo . . .' she moaned in a spooky voice.

'Yes, we're so terrified now,' said Jade, scornfully. She tossed her hair and turned away from the group, clutching her drink bottle and jacket.

Prani rolled her eyes. They were all used to this attitude from Jade.

One by one, the girls gathered their belongings and headed towards the carpark to their waiting parents.

Lily fell into step with Phoebe.

'I reckon this is pretty exciting, don't you?' Lily asked.

Phoebe nodded.

'I wonder what your clue will be. I can't wait to find out!'

Phoebe smiled.

'It's going to be huge fun! See ya!'

Chapter Seven

'What have you got that on for?'

It was moments before their game began on Saturday, and Phoebe's dad was peppering her with questions.

'Janet wants me to be Goal Keeper today.'

'Well, that's ridiculous!' Dad scoffed, loudly enough for everyone to hear. 'You shouldn't be in defence; you're the best goaler on the team. Come on, let's fix this.'

Phoebe felt herself being swept along with

her dad, who was heading towards Janet. When he had an idea in his head, it was hard to get him to listen.

'Wait, Dad,' she said, trying to slow him down so that she could explain. 'Everyone has to try different positions. I'm sure Janet will give me a different one later in the game, or next week.'

To her relief, she saw her dad pause.

'Fair enough,' he said, nodding. 'Why didn't you say so?'

Phoebe sighed. Sometimes it wasn't easy to get a word in with her dad!

'Well, you go out there, my zlata, and be the best defender you can be!'

Phoebe loved it when her dad called her his 'zlata'. It was a Croatian endearment that meant 'golden girl'.

As Phoebe trotted into position on court, Dad began cheering. 'Okay! Let's go, Marrang

Gems! Show them what you've got!' And the game hadn't even started yet!

The umpire's whistle blew and Phoebe's dad took up prime position, midway along the sidelines. He always made a point of encouraging all of the girls, not just Phoebe. He knew each of the players' names.

'Be ready, Isabella!' he called to Isabella, who was playing Goal Defence. 'Come on!'

Phoebe looked over to Isabella who looked a little startled at Phoebe's dad's enthusiasm.

Oh no, thought Phoebe. *He's weirded her out!* Phoebe watched anxiously to see what he'd do next. *Dad, please don't say anything else!*

But just then, Phoebe saw movement out of the corner of her eye. The ball landed in her opponent's hands. She hadn't even seen it coming!

'Phoebe, concentrate!'

Phoebe jumped at the sound of her dad's voice. She ran after the Burra Goal Shooter and into the goal circle. She stepped back, ready to put her arms up to defend, but she was too late! The ball was already sailing high through the air and the goal was scored.

This is a disaster! Phoebe thought.

'Don't worry, Phoebe.' Her dad's voice came from right beside her. He had moved down the sideline with the play. 'Just remember your training. You can do this.'

Her dad was right. Phoebe knew she could play better than this. *I need to stop worrying about Dad and the rest of the team and just focus on what I need to do.* She tried to think about what Janet had taught them at training. She had told them to stand close to their player – so close that their bodies touched. This was allowed as long as the other player didn't have the ball in her hands. Janet also taught them to stand side-on to their player, so that their opponent's shoulder was near their chest.

Phoebe decided to try it. She stood right up close to her opponent's side, between her and the goal post.

Hey, this really works, thought Phoebe. *I can see my player* and *the ball as it comes towards us!*

This time, when the Burra Wing Attack tried to pass the ball to the Goal Shooter, Phoebe was able to lean forward and tap it away towards Isabella, who was poised nearby, in the goal circle. She felt a rush of excitement when Isabella grabbed the ball and threw it up the court to Prani, who was playing Centre.

Phoebe was determined to try the same move again – and she did. Several more times she was able to stop the ball coming in to the Burra Goal Shooter. Eventually her opponent realised that she had to keep moving if she was going to get the ball while Phoebe was defending her!

As the game progressed, Phoebe became more and more engrossed in the play. Her father's yells and cheers from the sideline receded into the background. She found that she was able to anticipate what the Burra Goal Shooter would do because Phoebe often tried the same moves when she was a goaler. But now that she was defending, she could see what moves worked to get away from a defender. She locked those moves away in her mind to remember for the next time she was playing Goal Shooter or Goal Attack.

I'm learning so much about being a goaler by playing in defence! thought Phoebe. *I bet Dad will be surprised when I tell him!*

Chapter Eight

'Great work, Phoebe,' said Janet, when the team came off court at half-time. 'Are you okay to stay as Goal Keeper for the second half?'

Phoebe nodded happily.

'Well look at you!' Dad exclaimed. 'Beating them in defence as well! Come over here for a minute and I'll give you a few moves you can try.'

Phoebe went to follow her dad but Janet intervened. 'Phoebe, where are you going?'

'It's okay, Janet,' said Dad. 'I'm just going to give her a few tips.'

'Thanks, Bill,' Janet responded, politely but firmly, looking him straight in the eye, 'but I'm about to speak to the team, and Phoebe is part of that team.'

Phoebe looked anxiously at her dad. He opened his mouth in surprise – but didn't seem to know what to say. Phoebe knew it was almost impossible for him not to be actively involved in coaching and cheering her. It would kill him to stand back quietly while someone else advised her. But he had always told her and Max to respect the coach and the umpire, so he nodded to Phoebe to go with Janet.

Janet turned away and called the team into a huddle to discuss tactics for the second half. Phoebe stood on the outskirts of the team circle, half-facing her dad, not wanting to let him down.

When it was time to go back on court, Phoebe glanced across at her dad and was relieved to see that he had gathered himself and was standing ready to cheer for the Marrang Gems. In fact, he had already started pacing up and down along the sideline, once again calling out encouragement to different players before the game had even started!

The whistle blew and the second half began. Again, though, Phoebe found it hard to concentrate: as soon as the quarter had started, her dad had increased his pace. Phoebe watched as he trotted and shuffled along the side of the court in pace with the play.

What is he doing? wondered Phoebe, as she watched her dad.

Then she felt a hand pat her lightly on the back and a friendly voice beside her. 'Let's go, Phoebe.'

It was Lily. Phoebe smiled at her gratefully. She took a deep breath and turned back to the game. As the ball came down the court, she focused on trying to stop the Burra Goal Shooter from getting it. It still felt strange to follow her player instead of trying to get away from her, but Phoebe was determined to play as best she could. She worked hard to use her skills to catch rebounds from the goal ring throughout the third and fourth quarters.

In the final minutes of the game, the Burra Goal Shooter attempted a goal, but the ball bounced high off the ring.

This one's mine!

The Burra goalers had jumped too early, and they dropped away as Phoebe swung around, leapt up and snatched the ball out of the air. She fed it out to Lily in Wing Defence, who wasted no time passing it down to Maddy as Centre, who threw it to Sienna in Wing

Attack. Sienna passed it on, and it landed safely with Jade, the Goal Shooter, who converted it into a goal.

Lily spun around and high-fived Phoebe in delight. 'Great rebound, Phoebs!'

Phoebe tried to act cool and grin back, but her eyes were shining. Lily had called her 'Phoebs'. No one had ever given her a nickname before.

Just as the teams were positioning themselves for the next centre pass, the final whistle blew. The Gems had won! Phoebe joined her teammates in cheering, but they also remembered to shake hands with the Burra players.

'Good game.'

'Well played.'

Lily whispered in Phoebe's ear as they walked off the court. 'Isabella and Jade got an envelope each. Two more clues! Can you stay around for a little while so we can all look at them?'

Phoebe nodded – but then her dad appeared in front of her. 'How about all of those intercepts!' He wrapped her in a big bear hug. 'Now, off to the soccer to see some of Max's magic!'

Chapter Nine

Oh, no! I forgot about Max's game! How can I explain that I don't want to go?

Phoebe really didn't want to go over the whole story about the mystery puzzle. It was important to her because it felt like it was the one thing that tied her to her teammates. But if she took the time to explain all that to her dad, she might miss the whole thing!

'Um . . . Dad, I want to stay around the club for a while,' she said.

Her dad's expression changed from smiling to frowning instantly. 'You don't want to come to support your brother, even though he comes to support you?'

'It's not that,' Phoebe hastened to reassure him. 'I wanted to watch one of the senior games to . . . um . . . to see if I can pick up any skills. I can walk home later,' she added hopefully.

Dad nodded in agreement. 'Okay, my zlata, but make sure you don't get home too late.' He kissed her gently on the head, turned and headed for his car.

Phoebe watched for a moment, feeling a little guilty about not telling her dad the whole story, but then, when the coast was clear, she spun on her heel and raced towards the clubrooms, where the rest of the team was heading. She felt a zing of excitement at the idea of a mystery to solve.

Inside the clubrooms, all the girls clustered around a table against one of the windows.

Lily pulled a crumpled square of paper out of a pocket in her tracksuit pants and put it on the table. Sienna placed her square there, too.

'Before we see the next clues, maybe we should read the riddle again, just to be sure we didn't miss anything,' Lily suggested.

Jade read it aloud.

'Here is a puzzle to be solved by you,
when you are all down at the court.
Look out for a clue, or maybe two;
don't rush, give it plenty of thought!'

As soon as she finished reading, Jade placed her square on the table. It had lots of letters, but none of them made any sense!

ed to
arty
ugust at

Everyone stared at this new clue, their eyes travelling from one square to the other.

'Quick, Isabella, add your clue!' Maddy said.

Isabella carefully placed her clue next to the others.

arrang.
e celebrity.
over.

There was a burst of excited babble. A celebrity was involved!

Maddy began to shuffle the squares around, trying to match them up so that they made sense. Charlotte helped her, shifting the four squares around to see which combination worked. The rest of the team looked on, offering suggestions, which made their puzzle-solving even slower!

After a few tries, Jade yelled, 'Stop there! That's it! Look!'

You	ed to	a	arrang.
Birth	arty	on	e celebrity.
Sunda	ugust at	2.00 pm	over.

Prani jumped up and down on the spot. 'Yay! A birthday party! With a celebrity!' Wide-eyed, she breathed, 'Imagine if someone famous was there . . . Ooh, even better – imagine if it was a famous person's party!'

Jade cut her off with a wave of her hand. 'Come off it, Prani. As if the whole team would be invited to a famous person's party.' She smirked. 'Especially since *I'm* the only one here who actually knows a celebrity.'

Phoebe mentally rolled her eyes. They had all heard before about Jade's cousin who had been on *Big Brother*. But she looked down at the four clues, again. It *did* seem to be about a birthday party – and it *did* say 'celebrity'.

We just need more clues, she decided. *Hmm . . . More clues . . .*

'There might be more clues if we turn the cards over,' spoke Phoebe, quietly. 'Maybe there's some colour on the back of the new squares.'

Several of the girls were talking at once, so most of them didn't hear Phoebe. But Maddy, who was standing next to Phoebe, did. With a much louder voice, she called out, 'Turn the cards over!'

Phoebe was right. The new clues *did* have colour on the back! A new urgency fell on the girls, and they all leant in closer to examine the other side of each square.

'Oh my God,' Isabella exclaimed, waving both hands at the cards. 'Can anyone else see that? I reckon it's a photo – look! That bit is hair, and that bit could be part of a nose . . . or maybe an ear.'

Maddy and Lily tilted their heads and squinted.

'Or maybe a chin,' said Maddy.

'It's definitely a photo, though,' added Lily.

Finally they agreed to rack their brains over the next few days to see if they could crack the message. Lily, Sienna, Jade and Isabella each took back their clues, but as they all wandered out to watch the Under 17s play, they couldn't help but continue to speculate about the team mystery.

Chapter Ten

At the beginning of training the following Wednesday, Phoebe took off her jacket and put it on the bench near her water bottle. She was just retying her ponytail when she saw Maddy run up to join the group.

'I got a clue! I got a clue!'

Charlotte bounded over. 'Me too!'

'Really? Awesome!'

'Give us a look!'

'Nah, we should wait until everyone's here, otherwise Sienna will miss out.'

'I've been thinking about this and I reckon . . .'

'Where did I put it? . . .'

Everyone was talking at once. The excitement was contagious. Prani and Isabella started dancing on the spot, and Lily and Maddy chanted over and over, 'Let's do it now! Let's do it now!'

Phoebe stood nearby, staring at a pebble on the ground in front of her. *What if I don't get a clue? What if whoever's sending the mystery clues doesn't like me?* She took a deep breath, trying to shrug off the thought.

'Okay, girls,' called Janet, once Sienna had arrived. 'Come over here so we can start.'

But everyone was so caught up in the clues that no one heard!

'Girls!' Janet shouted. This time she had a

very serious expression on her face. 'Right. Listen carefully because I do not want to have to repeat this. Obviously there's something exciting going on, but you all know that while we are training or playing a match, you need to listen to me and pay attention. Do you understand?' She glared at the girls.

Phoebe swallowed nervously. She distinctly heard a loud gulp from Prani.

Janet grinned suddenly. 'But make sure you tell me what it is when the mystery's solved!'

The girls' eyes lit up. Even Janet wanted to know what the mystery was!

Janet then sent the whole team for a warm-up lap of the football ground that was next to the netball courts. It began as a subdued jog for the first hundred metres, but Sienna bounced back quickly from being told off. She took something out of her pocket with a flourish. To everyone's delight, she pulled on a pair of huge red sunglasses. At each corner of the glasses, there was a green plastic parrot perched high, poking into her hair.

She playfully jiggled them up and down on her nose. When she spoke, she drew out each word slowly for effect. 'I *reeeally* need these today, because this way, I can check out those boys over there at footy training!'

At that, all eyes turned towards the large group of boys kicking footballs in a complicated drill that covered the entire stretch of grass.

Phoebe turned back to watch Sienna, and chuckled when she saw that Sienna was now somehow wearing the glasses upside down.

They jogged slowly. All of the girls were more interested in Sienna's glasses and the boys at training than in focusing on their warm-up.

Suddenly, one of the red footballs the boys were kicking around rolled under the fence, right in front of Phoebe. Phoebe stopped to pick it up, then passed it from one hand to the other, looking to see who had kicked it out.

'Here! Kick it to me!' one of the boys called from the goal posts.

Phoebe smiled and kicked the ball over the fence to the blond-haired boy who had his arms raised.

'Thanks, Phoebe! See you at the fete!' he called. He waved at her and then turned away, kicking the ball towards one of the other boys.

Phoebe turned to start jogging again, but quickly noticed that every girl in her team had stopped and was staring at the boy. Then, one by one, their focus shifted until all of them were staring at Phoebe. She looked back, puzzled by the sudden silence. It didn't last long.

'Who's *he*?'

'What's his *name*?'

'How do you *know* him?'

'Do you know any of the *others*?'

Phoebe started walking, surrounded by her teammates, who were peppering her with questions.

'That's just Jordan,' she replied, shrugging a shoulder. She was a bit stunned to be at the centre of attention. 'He's my brother's friend. He comes over to our house all the time.'

'Oh, you lucky thing!' Jade said, sighing.

'He's *sooo* cute!' said Sienna.

'Do you like him?' asked Prani.

Phoebe shrugged both shoulders this time. 'Sure. He's nice.'

Prani giggled. 'No, we mean, do you *like* like him?'

Phoebe blushed. She answered 'Not really' – but was so quiet that no one actually heard her answer. They started to tease her.

'You *looove* him!'

'You want to *kiiiss* him!'

'You want to *maaarry* him!'

Prani made loud kissing noises in Pheobe's right ear, then Lily wrapped her arms around her, forcing her to stop walking. 'Oh Jordan, I love you *sooo* much!' she said, in a squeaky-high extra-girly voice.

Phoebe grinned, shoving Lily away. She glanced over her shoulder to check that Jordan was out of hearing range. If he heard them, she would absolutely die from embarrassment. Every time he came over to see her brother, she'd have to hide in her bedroom. Luckily he was too far away to have heard.

Phoebe turned back around, relieved. 'Well, if you're going to the fete, you can see him there,' she said.

'In that case, I'm going to be at the fete all day!' said Jade.

Phoebe smiled and took in what was happening.

For the very first time – finally! – she was really in the middle of this group.

Not on the side looking in.

Not feeling too shy.

In the middle.

The only thing was that all the girls were so wrapped up in their conversation that they hadn't noticed Janet approaching from behind! One by one, they spotted her frowning behind Phoebe, and their faces sobered up, guiltily.

Lily, unaware, continued to squeal at Phoebe. 'But I *caaan't* live without you!'

'Well,' said Janet, 'if you get moving on the warm-up, you *won't* have to live without her!'

Lily screwed her face up when she heard her mother's tone. She gave her a small wave, then turned to start jogging, muttering to everyone. 'Just run. Trust me. Don't say another word!'

Chapter Eleven

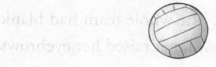

During the passing drills, the usually loud chatter was absent. The girls felt guilty about not doing the warm-up run properly and wanted to show Janet that they were not going to muck around anymore. Each girl concentrated on passing the ball straight to her partner.

Janet nodded approvingly when she called them to gather together again. 'Today we are going to be doing a drill so that you can practise leading out for a centre pass. "Leading out" means that when the whistle blows, you move in front of your opponent so that you're free to take the centre pass. For our practice, I want you to line up behind the transverse line in pairs.'

No one moved. The whole team had blank looks on their faces. Janet raised her eyebrows at the group.

Phoebe was too shy to ask Janet what she meant. She knew that Janet had explained this a few weeks ago, and that she should remember what the transverse lines were.

'Um . . . Mum . . . Which one is the trans-whatever line, again?'

Phoebe was relieved that Lily had spoken up.

'Oh, sorry,' Janet replied. 'I should have realised you might not remember.' She smiled at the group of girls. 'The transverse lines are the lines that divide the court into thirds,' she explained, 'which means that there are two of them.' She pointed to the nearest one. 'That's the transverse line I'd like you to line up behind.'

Understanding dawned on the faces of all the girls. They headed to where Janet pointed.

'Okay, now decide with your partner who will be the attacker and who will be the defender.'

While each pair decided this, Janet grabbed a netball. She stood in the centre circle.

'When I call "play", the attacker will run forward in a straight line to try to catch the ball I pass you. Defenders, you stick with your partner. You might even manage to intercept a pass.'

Phoebe and Charlotte were the first to try. When Janet called 'play', Charlotte, who was attacking, attempted to run in a straight line towards Janet. Phoebe ran with her. When

Janet passed the ball, Phoebe stretched her arm in front of Charlotte and tapped the ball away so that Charlotte couldn't grab it.

'Good try, Charlotte. Nice work, Phoebe. Okay, next.'

Once each pair had a turn, the partners swapped roles. Phoebe began to notice that some attackers attempted different strategies to break free.

'Okay. We'll stop there,' said Janet. 'I noticed that we started with a straight lead, which was good. That's what I wanted. But when that didn't work, what did you do instead?'

'I tried to change direction.'

'I dodged a bit.'

'I ran out wider.'

'Exactly,' said Janet. 'Even though I wanted you to practise a straight lead, I was impressed that you tried other things when that tactic didn't work. Well done, everyone.' Janet paused for a moment and glanced at Jade. 'What did you try, Jade?'

'I dropped back for a lob pass,' Jade replied, confident as always.

'Yes. Does anyone know why that might not always be a good idea?'

Jade's superior smirk faded when she realised that she may have done something wrong, but Janet noticed and hastened to reassure her. 'It *can* be a very good move sometimes, Jade.'

Isabella raised her hand to answer Janet's question. 'Um . . . You could have a tall player on you, and she could jump and get the pass?'

'That's exactly right.'

For the rest of the practice session, all the girls tried extra hard with everything Janet asked them to do. They didn't dare talk about the mystery. But Phoebe couldn't help sneakily checking her watch. She could hardly wait for training to finish so they could see what Maddy and Charlotte's clues were.

There was just one thing still bothering her, and it had niggled at her mind all throughout the training session. So far, six of the girls had been sent clues. Phoebe and Prani were the only ones on the team who hadn't received one.

What if it ends up that I'm the only one who doesn't get a clue?

Chapter Twelve

When training had finished, every one of the girls headed to the clubrooms. Usually they mucked around, shooting goals, until one by one they headed home. Lily and Janet were always the last to leave. This week, however, with hasty excuses of a 'team meeting', they had about ten minutes to see if they could solve the riddle with the help of the latest two mystery clues.

Charlotte and Maddy didn't waste any time putting their clues down on the table next to the four they already had. Lily muttered loudly enough for everyone to hear, as she puzzled over the words.

Maddy's clue read:

> at
> Dress
> Whose

Charlotte's square revealed whole words as well:

> M
> favourit
> Flip me

'Flip me?' Prani giggled. 'Maybe we have to do gymnastics for a celebrity!' She bent backwards until her hands reached the ground behind her and flipped her legs over one at a time. She righted herself and flung her arms above her head. 'Tada!'

Maddy jumped in to have a go as well, but her backwards flip was much less successful than Prani's. She ended up sprawled in the corner, laughing.

'Don't forget the finish!' Prani reminded her.

Maddy sprang up. 'Tada!' they yelled in unison, their arms flung wide.

Completely ignoring them, Lily kept muttering to herself, trying to work out where the two new clues should fit in with the others.

'Well, now it's starting to make a bit of sense,' said Jade.

You	ed to	a
birth	arty	on
Sunda	ugust at	2.00 pm

at	M	arrang.
Dress	favourit	e celebrity.
Whose	Flip me	over.

'We can sort of guess what most of the message might be – it's a birthday party, somewhere in Marrang,' Maddy mused.

'But what on earth does "Flip me over" mean?' said Lily.

Just at that moment, Janet stuck her head around the doorway. 'Girls! What are you up to? Your parents are asking where I've hidden you all!'

Everyone jumped in surprise. They had been so engrossed in the puzzle clues that they'd forgotten where they were!

As they scrambled to pick up their belongings, Sienna shoved all the clues into her sports bag. 'I'll keep them until next week, okay?' she asked.

Everyone agreed, but Jade delivered a parting comment as she started running towards her mum's car. 'If you lose them, Sienna, I'll flip *you* over – and leave you upside down!'

Chapter Thirteen

Two nights later, Phoebe settled blissfully into the cosy folds of the couch. Her parents were getting ready to go out. Max was playing on the computer. She had the TV all to herself and had prepared some drinks and snacks. She knew Caitlyn would be arriving soon to look after them and had chosen a movie they could watch together.

'Phoebe! I almost forgot!' Dad bustled in, dressed for dinner but still with bare feet and unbrushed hair. He picked up the DVD remote and started jabbing at the buttons and muttering in frustration. Nothing changed on the TV.

'Dad, what are you doing?'

'Australia's playing New Zealand – Diamonds versus Silver Ferns. I thought you'd want to watch the game,' he said, as he frowned at the remote, then up at the TV.

'But I've already picked a movie to watch,' said Phoebe.

'This will be much better . . . Urghh! This stupid thing never works!'

Phoebe giggled. Dad had no idea when it came to any form of technology. Once she had even seen him pick up the TV remote to answer the phone!

'Dad, that's the wrong remote,' she said.

The doorbell rang.

'Max, can you answer the door?' Dad

bellowed. But after a few moments had passed, it was obvious that even Dad's voice couldn't penetrate Max's concentration when he was playing computer games.

'I'll get it,' said Phoebe, and she went to let Caitlyn in.

Caitlyn was six years older than Phoebe, but Phoebe always felt relaxed with her. She seemed happy to watch the TV shows Phoebe and Max liked, and now that Phoebe had started playing netball, Caitlyn was always willing to give her tips and have a practice game.

'Got it!' said Dad, when Phoebe walked back into the lounge room, followed by Caitlyn.

'Hello, Caitlyn!' said Dad. 'Have a seat. The game's just started. Now Phoebe – this is the player you need to watch . . .'

Dad stood up, pointing out the Australian goalers and leaning in to check their names, which were written on the back of their uniforms. He was so enthusiastic that he kept shuffling closer and closer to the TV. Squinting to read the words, he completely blocked the screen so that Phoebe and Caitlyn couldn't see a thing! The girls grinned at each other.

'Watch the Goal Shooter, Phoebe. See the way she keeps working the ball out to the Wing Attack until she's close under the ring? Can't miss from there,' he said, watching and admiring the players.

'It would help if we could see through you!' said Caitlyn, laughing.

'Bill, we're running late,' Mum called out from the bedroom. Dad stepped back from the screen, reluctantly.

'Watch it, Phoebe,' he urged. 'You can learn a lot from these players.'

Phoebe had really wanted to watch the movie she had picked, but now the netball game was on, she had to admit that her dad knew her well. This was *way* better than any movie!

'Okay, Dad,' said Phoebe. 'Do you mind, Caitlyn?'

'No, I love watching the Diamonds play!'

Chapter Fourteen

Finally Mum and Dad left and the house was quiet.

Phoebe tried to watch the Australian goalers as Dad had suggested, but her eyes kept being drawn to the Goal Attack playing for the New Zealand Silver Ferns. Her movements were just so smooth and graceful, and she was unfazed by the constant jostling of the Australian defenders. She would shoot for goal from wherever she was standing, and it seemed that the ball glided through the goal ring every time, barely skimming the sides as it went.

The Australian Diamonds were winning the game, for which Phoebe was glad. Secretly, though, she cheered every time the New Zealand Goal Attack got the ball and scored again. She didn't want to admit it to Caitlyn, though, in case she thought Phoebe was being disloyal to Australia.

At the half-time break, Australia was leading by seven goals. Caitlyn wandered off to get herself another drink and to check on Max. Phoebe stayed in front of the TV, wanting to know the name of the goaler she'd been watching.

As they displayed a table of the goaling percentages, the commentators discussed the results. 'Maria Tutaia, of course, is in Goal Attack for New Zealand. She's a very consistent player, shooting at 95% accuracy tonight.'

Phoebe knew this meant that Maria Tutaia was getting almost every goal.

Maria Tutaia, Maria Tutaia, Phoebe repeated the name to herself. *I want to play like her!*

Caitlyn wandered back into the room and plonked her cup of tea down on the table. 'So who's your favourite player in the game?' she asked Phoebe.

Phoebe hesitated, unsure if she should admit to favouring a New Zealander. She shrugged noncommittally.

'Well,' said Caitlyn, 'I have to admit that whenever Maria Tutaia's on court, I'm cheering for her. She's awesome!'

'I know!' said Phoebe. 'She's amazing!'

When the third quarter commenced, Phoebe curled her legs up underneath her, keen to watch Maria Tutaia again.

'That shooting action,' Caitlyn murmured, as they watched Maria put another goal through the ring.

Phoebe nodded silently in agreement, not daring to look away from the screen in case she missed anything.

They continued to watch the game together, both completely absorbed. It was an exciting finish, with a clear win to New Zealand, who had come from behind.

Caitlyn turned to Phoebe. 'Want to try to shoot like Maria Tutaia?'

It was too dark to go outside and practise, so while they waited for the popcorn to pop, they stood up in front of the couch and mimicked the way Maria held her arms when she went for a goal.

went through her last-minute ritual. It always helped to steady her nerves before the game. First she tightened her ponytail, then she adjusted her shoelaces – left foot first, then

Chapter Fifteen

It was time. Her moment had finally come.
The mood in the stadium was electric. Everyone knew how tough this game was going to
be, for both teams.

Phoebe's nerves were tingling. As she stood
on court, waiting for the whistle to blow, she
went through her last-minute ritual. It always
helped to steady her nerves before the game.
First she tightened her ponytail, then she
adjusted her shoelaces – left foot first, then

right – and, finally, she bounced on her toes to loosen the tension in her muscles.

The whistle went and the game exploded into action. Phoebe stood poised, ready for anything. Australia had the first centre pass and moved the ball quickly into their goal third. But Phoebe's teammates were ready for them. The New Zealand defenders put pressure on every pass. They quickly intercepted the ball and sent it down towards their team's goal circle. Seeing the turn of play, both the Australian defenders rushed back to defend Phoebe, the New Zealand Goal Shooter. She was blocked at every turn!

Just then, Maria flew into the goal circle. She took a pass from the New Zealand Wing Attack and turned to shoot for goal. But as soon as it left her hand, Phoebe knew it wouldn't make it. It was very rare for Maria to miss, but Phoebe was right. The ball rebounded high off the ring. Phoebe was determined to catch it. She paused deliberately and waited until the last possible moment, then she soared into the air and just managed to tip the ball up and out of the defender's hands. Snatching the ball for herself, Phoebe quickly popped it through for the first goal of the game.

One section of the crowd – the section where everyone was dressed in black and white – roared. 'Sil-ver Ferns! Sil-ver Ferns!'

Maria Tutaia turned to Phoebe and, with a wide smile, gave her a high five before turning back to be ready for the next centre pass. Phoebe grinned in delight at their successful start. She was buzzing with energy, but told herself to keep focused.

This time it was New Zealand's centre pass. The ball was heading their way. Phoebe, all senses alert, saw Maria head to the top of the goal circle. This left room for Phoebe to run along the baseline, where she took a high pass from the Wing Attack. When she turned, though, she realised that she wasn't close enough to the goal ring to make an easy shot.

'Here if you need!' she heard her team's Centre call from behind. Phoebe paused, unsure if she should pass it out or try for a goal.

'Go for it!' Maria said, standing ready under the goal ring for any rebounds.

That was all Phoebe needed. She swung the ball up and sent it flying towards the ring in one smooth action.

It made it! The Silver Ferns were on fire!

The Australian defenders were getting desperate. For the rest of the game, they crowded and blocked Phoebe and Maria, but it was as though they could read each other's minds — both of them knew when to pass to a space just before the other reached it, or whether to go for a goal or pass it to the other.

Finally the whistle sounded and the game was over. The New Zealand supporters cheered as loudly as they could. Phoebe and Maria had both scored with over 95% accuracy, and had won the game for the Silver Ferns!

'Phoebe!'

She could hear people in the crowd calling for her autograph.

'Phoebe! Phoebe, are you listening?'

Phoebe reluctantly turned around and saw her mother looking at her quizzically. The whole stadium immediately vanished.

'Phoebe, it's almost time to head down to the fete. Best come in and get ready now.'

Phoebe nodded, wondering if her mum had noticed anything while she had been practising in the backyard.

'Oh Phoebe – one more thing. Did you win for Australia?' Mum asked, with a little smile.

'Yeah, sure, Mum,' said Phoebe, rolling her eyes, pretending her mum was way off.

Thank goodness she doesn't know who I was really playing for!

Chapter Sixteen

The voices of the crowd, the tinny music of the rides and the flapping of the marquees drifted towards Phoebe and her family on the breeze. They were approaching the gates of the school grounds where the fete was being held. The fete was organised by the Marrang community and involved four of the local schools, including Phoebe's.

Phoebe stood for a moment at the gates, absorbing the spectacle of colour and movement and working out where she should start first. But her family were already heading off in three different directions!

'I'd better get going,' said Mum. 'I promised Marj I'd help at the second-hand-toy stall.'

'Here's some money for rides, kids,' said Dad, as he handed them each a generous amount. 'I'm supposed to be on the spinning wheel, so I'd better head off.' Dad had volunteered to be in charge of working the large spinning wheel. It had numbers around the edges and people bought tickets to guess the number it would stop at. They won a prize if their guess was correct. The organisers obviously knew that Dad's booming voice would be perfect for calling out the winning numbers!

'See ya,' Max said to Phoebe, with a wave. He had spotted Jordan and his other mates already getting soaked in a water fight. They were stalking each other from behind and between the marquees. Some of the adults nearby didn't look too pleased – they were getting wet in the crossfire!

Phoebe was left looking awkwardly around. Suddenly she was on her own and the fete didn't seem as much fun. She felt as if she was the only person there who wasn't hanging out with friends or family. She didn't want to look as if she didn't have anyone to hang out with, though, so she walked purposefully towards one of the stalls, which had handmade jewellery and ornaments on display. She used some of the money her dad had given her to buy a hand-painted wooden bangle. She had really only bought it for something to do, but when she put it on, she admired it as it hung from her wrist. It was bright and colourful, and reminded her of the cheerful bangles that Prani wore.

She turned and spotted the rides on the oval.

There was an inflatable jumping castle, the bungee tramps, and something called the Storm Twister. Phoebe bought some ride tickets from the ticket booth and then wandered over to get a closer look. People were being strapped into harnesses in a carriage that tipped and twisted and spun until everyone was screaming. It looked terrifying, but absolutely awesome!

'Hey Phoebe!'

Phoebe turned around and saw Jade and Isabella waiting a long way down the queue that snaked away from the entry gate to the Storm Twister. They were waving for her to come over. Phoebe felt her whole body relax. For the first time since arriving, she felt like she was part of the crowd. She hurried over.

'What's happening?' Jade asked her. 'Have you seen Jordan yet?'

'He's with Max. I just got here,' Phoebe replied.

'I heard you lost against Waroona yesterday,' said Jade.

'Yeah, they were all really, really tall and really, really good,' said Phoebe.

'You needed me there to help with goaling,' said Jade, smirking. 'Pity I was at a birthday party.'

Phoebe looked away and didn't answer.

'Did you see Sienna doing SingStar on stage?' said Isabella, kindly changing the subject. 'It was hilarious!'

Phoebe laughed. She could just imagine Sienna being brave enough to do that. 'There's no way I could do that,' Phoebe said quietly. 'What are the rides like?'

'I guess we're about to find out,' said Jade, smartly, 'but don't think you're going to cut into the line. You have go to the end and wait like the rest of us.'

Phoebe looked at her in shock. She turned

to Isabella to check with her but Isabella clearly wasn't going to speak up against Jade.

'Sorry,' Isabella mouthed to Phoebe.

Phoebe turned away. Embarrassed, she headed with eyes down towards the end of the line. It was so long that it had begun to curve and turn back on itself. Phoebe stepped in behind a group of three young boys at the end.

Is the ride even going to be worth it? she thought. *I look so stupid standing here by myself. Maybe I should just help Mum at the toy stall . . .*

Chapter Seventeen

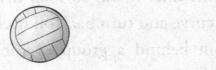

'Phoebe! Phoebe!'

Phoebe turned at the sound of her name. Lily was calling to her from near the front of the line to the Storm Twister. Prani and Sienna were just ahead of her. Prani was waving her arms, her bangles clinking musically together.

It was nice to hear Lily's friendly voice. Phoebe stood and waved to Lily, Prani and Sienna but didn't move towards them. She wouldn't make that mistake again.

'Come over here!' Lily called to her. 'You can jump in with us!'

Sienna gave Phoebe a broad smile and stepped back, making room for her. 'You're just in time. We're about to go on.'

Should I go over to them? wondered Phoebe. *I want to . . . And they all seem a lot nicer than Jade.*

Hesitating for a moment longer, Phoebe took a deep, shaky breath, then started to move towards her teammates. When she got there, Prani started jumping around on the spot, swinging her head at weird angles.

'Prani, what are you doing?' Sienna asked.

'I'm getting ready for the ride, but it's making me feel a little dizzy!' she said, giggling and stumbling slightly.

'We're on!' Lily announced, and the four of them leapt through the gates and raced to claim a four-seat booth.

Phoebe fastened her harness, her heart thumping. The ride started and as the spinning got faster and faster, she felt the skin tighten on her face. She held on tightly. There was no space for talk. Phoebe felt as if she had to use all her concentration just to hold on! When the carriage began to jerk and change direction, she opened her mouth and, along with the other girls, screamed continuously in both fear and exhilaration.

When the ride finally came to a stop, Phoebe's legs were trembling. She stumbled along with the others out onto the oval.

Prani looked a little stunned. 'Well, my head-swinging didn't get me ready for *that*!' she said.

The others looked at her and burst out laughing.

'Hot chips?' she suggested, and they headed off to the hot-chips stand.

As they walked past the marquees, Phoebe heard Lily squeal in surprise. At the very same time, she felt a blast of cold hit her right in the middle of her back.

'Ahhh!'

She turned to see what was happening and spotted Max, Jordan and two of their mates peering around a marquee holding water pistols. All four girls stood still, the backs of their clothes dripping.

Sienna gathered herself first. 'Quick. Run!'

She sprinted towards the safety of the school hall, followed by Lily, Prani and Phoebe. The boys were in hot pursuit but the girls made it, landing, gasping, inside the doors just in time.

'Nuuumber eighty-six! Eighty-six! Does anyone have lucky number eighty-six?' Phoebe's dad's voice boomed through the microphone. He was standing right next to the girls, calling out the winning numbers on the spinning wheel.

'Phoebe!' said Dad. 'Just the girl I need! Can you help me collect money for the tickets? There are more people here than I thought there would be.'

'But Dad!' said Phoebe. She had only just started having fun with the other girls!

Dad raised his eyebrows. 'Phoebe. This is for a good cause.'

Phoebe was conscious of the girls watching. Her face flushed red. 'Okay.' She sighed and dutifully took the money tin from her dad, then turned to watch the girls moving away. With a quick wave, they bounced off through the hall.

Phoebe attempted a smile at her dad. He didn't mean to stop her making friends . . . But this was the first time she had hung out with Sienna, Prani and Lily. Would she get another chance? Would they even bother to include her next time?

Chapter Eighteen

Phoebe grabbed the mail from the letterbox as she came in through the front gate. She didn't look at the bundle of letters. She was too caught up in thoughts about training that night. She had seen dark clouds looming overhead on her walk home from the bus stop. It wasn't raining at the moment and she didn't know if she wanted it to start or not. She wanted to see her teammates again, but she didn't think she could bear going to training and listening to the others talk about the fete. She didn't want to feel left out again.

She tossed the letters onto the kitchen bench. One square white envelope slipped away from the pile of bills. Phoebe stared at it. It was addressed to her! Holding her breath in hope, she ripped it open. The familiar riddle fell out into her hand. Phoebe knew every word by heart, but she still read it with pleasure because this one was meant for her.

'Here is a puzzle to be solved by you,
when you are all down at the court.
Look out for a clue, or maybe two;
don't rush, give it plenty of thought!'

She looked back into the envelope and saw the puzzle piece sitting snugly in the corner, waiting for her.

'Mum! *Mum!* I got one!' Phoebe was so excited she couldn't contain herself. Her heart was racing and when she spotted her mum in the backyard, she rushed out to tell her the news.

'Mum, I got a clue!' she said breathlessly.

'Oh Phoebe, that's fantastic!'

Now Phoebe couldn't *wait* to get to training! *Please, rain, don't start now!* she thought.

But as soon as Phoebe and Mum got into the car, big, fat raindrops started landing on the windscreen.

'This doesn't look too promising,' Mum said, peering up at the sky.

Phoebe said nothing. She couldn't imagine Janet cancelling training for a few drops.

But as they drove, the spattering of the raindrops became heavier and more constant, and by the time they arrived at the courts, the rain was pelting down and the windscreen was awash. Phoebe could just make out the figures of Janet and Lily as they threw the training equipment back into their car, before jumping in themselves. There was no one else at the drenched courts. All Phoebe could see were the headlights of the other cars in the carpark, as they swung out and headed back home.

Phoebe looked out of the car window.

'Disappointed?' her mum asked kindly.

Phoebe said nothing. Then a moment later she blurted out, 'It's not fair. We were going to look at the clues together . . .'

'Don't worry. Your game is only three days away. You can show the others your clue then,' said Mum.

Yes, thought Phoebe, *the game isn't far away. I can wait until then.*

And then she smiled to herself again with the realisation that she hadn't been forgotten.

I got a clue!

Chapter Nineteen

'What's this?' Phoebe's dad asked, as her mum placed two thermoses and a tall stack of cups on the kitchen table.

'Some hot chocolate for the girls. Have you noticed how cold that wind can be when it blows onto the courts, up off the river?'

Phoebe's dad hadn't noticed, but of course he was always in a constant state of motion.

'Yum! Thanks, Mum,' said Phoebe. 'The girls will love it.'

'I thought it would be good timing, since you're taking your turn as team captain this week.'

Phoebe beamed at Mum. The prospect of being team captain had sat in her mind since Thursday night when Janet had called to tell her, and every time she had thought about it since then, she'd glowed with excitement.

'Well, let's get going then,' said Dad.

Phoebe grabbed her drink bottle and the precious clue. Mum gathered the hot chocolate and cups. Dad spent the next five minutes searching for the car keys. Then, just as they had all stepped out the door, Max realised that he was missing one of his soccer boots.

Finally they arrived at the courts. Phoebe hurried over to fill out the scoresheet. It was her first job as team captain. She checked with Janet where everyone was playing. When she listed herself as the Goal Attack, as Janet had told her to, she put a little smiley face in the 'o' of 'Phoebe'. Goal Attack! She was going to be playing in the same position as Maria Tutaia! She visualised Maria playing. She thought about Maria's fast but smooth movement down the court, and her . . .

Phoebe's thoughts were interrupted by the umpire, who appeared before her holding a coin in the palm of her hand. Phoebe's other job as team captain was to join the umpires and the opposition captain for the coin toss. The winner would get to decide whether they would choose their team's goal end, or whether to start with the ball. Phoebe proudly walked out onto the court with the umpire and smiled briefly at the small, red-haired Thomson team captain who joined them.

The Marrang Gems were the first-named team on the scoresheet, so Phoebe got to call the toss.

'Tails,' she called as the coin spun in the air. The umpire caught it and flipped it onto the back of her hand. It was tails!

'We'll take first centre pass,' said Phoebe, without hesitation. It was a still and overcast day and she knew it would be much the same goaling from either end of the court.

Phoebe joined her team.

Lily looked at her curiously. 'So who gets first centre pass?'

'We do!' said Phoebe, her eyes twinkling, 'and I've got a new clue for after the game!'

'Me too!' squealed Prani.

'Yay!' cried the team, and they turned and ran onto the court.

Phoebe felt good in her Goal Attack bib. As the first quarter wore on, she better under-stood her role. She knew she had to help bring the ball down the court, as well as help the Goal Shooter shoot goals.

Thomson had the next centre pass. Before their Goal Attack could catch the ball, Isabella in Goal Defence had leapt in front and snatched it out of the air. She quickly flicked it to Sienna in Wing Defence, who passed it straight on to Lily as Wing Attack. Phoebe readied herself for action, but was distracted when she sensed a flurry of activity on the sidelines of the court. She spun around to see what was happening. It was her dad! In his eagerness to follow the game, he was hurrying along the sidelines, calling out his encourage-ment to the players. The only problem was that he was getting in the way of the umpire!

Phoebe gestured to her dad to step back, and he looked around in surprise. He hadn't even noticed he was blocking the umpire! He stumbled backwards in haste. Phoebe glanced at Mum and Max, who were sitting on the bench by the court, smiling and shaking their heads, then winced as she saw the cross face of the umpire.

But the game was continuing, so she turned her attention to the court. Bit by bit, she began to settle back into the rhythm of the game. Maddy stepped into the centre circle, clasping the ball firmly in both hands. She nodded her head once at Lily, who nodded back. Lily was holding firm on the line, against the jostling of the Wing Defence. When the whistle sounded, Maddy ignored her Thomson Centre opponent, who waved her arms, hoping to deflect a pass. When Lily made a straight lead towards her, Maddy snapped her a quick pass and raced down court, to the edge of the goal circle.

Maddy called to Lily for the ball, then shouted out to Phoebe to prepare for the next catch. 'Go Phoebe!' she yelled.

Phoebe was ready. She sprang into action, sprinting towards the goal circle. She ran so fast that her Goal Defence opponent couldn't keep up with her! Jade, their Goal Shooter, was at the top of the goal circle, and she stood firmly against the Goal Keeper. Phoebe raced past her, glancing up just in time to catch the flying lob from Maddy.

Phoebe landed firmly on both feet, close to the goal ring, the ball in her hands. She took a precious second to correct her body position, then, raising her arms high above her head, she balanced the ball just like she'd seen Maria Tutaia do. Phoebe had no time to aim carefully at the goal ring. She had only one more second before the umpire called 'held ball'. She flicked the ball up at the ring.

It was a goal!

'Woohoo!'

'Yay Phoebe!'

Phoebe grinned as she heard the cheers of her dad, her coach and her team.

Chapter Twenty

Just after quarter time, the pace of the game increased. The Thomson netball team had swapped some of their players. It may have been because the new players were more skilled than those in the first quarter, or just because the team was settling into the game, but slowly the goals started to level.

The Thomson spectators, sensing the change in tempo on court, began to cheer more loudly. Phoebe's dad couldn't resist the opportunity to support his daughter and her team. He ran up and down along the sideline, yelling and cheering them on. Once again, Phoebe didn't know where to look – at the ball or at him.

Taking a sneaking glance at her dad, Phoebe saw him veer quickly to the left to avoid running into the umpire. He tripped over a sports bag in his path and pitched forward into a spectacular double somersault. He squashed three bags on landing and finally ended up flat on his back, staring up into the umpire's glaring face.

'*Brrrp*,' went the umpire's whistle. 'Injury time . . . for the spectator!'

'I'm okay, nothing to worry about here,' said Dad, as he struggled to his feet.

Phoebe went bright red with embarrassment. She couldn't look at any of her team-mates or her coach. She was pretty sure this

was the first time in history that injury time had been called for a spectator! She stared at her dad, stunned, and watched as her mum went to help him limp over to the first-aid room.

Janet called the girls in for a team huddle.

'Okay, minor distraction everyone. Now, we need to focus for the rest of the game. Thomson is a very good team and it's going to take a lot of hard work to beat them!'

'Minor? That was the biggest crash I've ever seen!' said Jade, laughing.

Phoebe cringed at the sound of the others laughing along with her.

After a pause, though, Jade added, 'Shame he had to go. He's the best cheer squad ever!'

Phoebe looked up in surprise. She had not expected that from Jade. To her relief, she could see everyone else agree.

'Yeah, he's awesome,' said Maddy.

'Okay, Phoebe?' Janet asked. 'If you can concentrate, I'll leave you as Goal Attack for the second half as well.'

'Thanks, Janet,' said Phoebe, nodding uncertainly.

Lily appeared beside her and smiled. 'Relax, Phoebe, you're so good at shooting.'

Phoebe smiled gratefully, and when the whistle went for play to resume, she allowed herself to get drawn back into the game. Soon, all she was thinking about was getting ready for the next pass, looking for the next free player, and shooting her next goal.

She didn't even see her dad returning to sit on the bench after half-time. Mum poured him a generous serve of hot chocolate. His elbow and knee were bandaged, but he still managed to call out encouragements from time to time. Phoebe didn't really hear. She was determined to show Janet just how well she could play in

Goal Attack. In her determination, she found herself in a place where everything outside the court was zoned out and for once she was able to play her best netball.

And she needed every bit of concentration she had. Both teams were straining to get in front of the other. By the final quarter, it was turning into a battle for the Marrang Gems to keep up with Thomson, a tough team that was used to winning.

Chapter Twenty-one

There was only one minute until the end of the game and the score was tied! The time-keeper stared fixedly at the timer, watching the final seconds pass. Maddy grabbed the ball and raced into the centre circle. She nodded at Phoebe, her signal to make a lead.

The whistle blew to start play. Phoebe burst forward and caught a fast low pass from Maddy. Turning, she ignored the teammates close to her, who were calling loudly for a pass – she had seen Jade waving at her from right under the goal post.

Can I throw that far? Will it work?

Making a split-second decision, Phoebe lifted her arms high. Using her shoulder muscles, she threw the ball as hard as she could, straight and fast all the way to the goal circle. Jade saw the ball bulleting towards her. She braced her feet, and the ball smacked into her hands.

The timekeeper was standing, ready to call time to the umpires . . . Jade turned to face the goal ring and confidently popped the ball through the ring.

'Time!' called the timekeeper. *Brrrp* went the umpire's whistle.

The Marrang players looked around at Janet, unsure which team had won the game. Then they saw her grinning and holding one finger in the air. The Marrang Gems had won by one goal!

Phoebe was totally pumped with the way she had played. It felt like it had been her best game yet.

As the team came off court, they buzzed with excitement. Charlotte, who had sat out the last half of the game, came from the bench to join the girls.

'Oh my God! That last quarter was so exciting! I didn't know who was going to win!'

Phoebe smiled at Charlotte. *It* was *pretty great!* she thought, as she watched her teammates all eagerly reaching for the hot chocolate her mum was handing out.

But the excitement of the day wasn't over. Phoebe and Prani still hadn't shown their clues to the others! Even though Phoebe knew what her clue said, she wasn't sure how it would fit into the puzzle. But she knew this much – they were very close to solving the mystery invitation.

Prani started to jump up and down on the spot. She waved her arms wildly at the group. 'Come *ooon*! Hurry up so we can put all the clues together and work out what the message says!'

She turned and ran madly towards the grass area behind the clubrooms and the rest of the team took off after her. They collapsed on the grass and looked at Sienna expectantly.

'Oh no, I forgot to bring the clues!' she said.

A chorus of horrified responses yelled at once.

'What?'

'No way!'

'You didn't!'

Sienna grinned. 'Only joking. Here they are!'

She placed the six clues they all knew on the grass in the middle of the circle and carefully arranged them in the order they had agreed upon.

Prani stretched over on her knees with her square of paper fluttering in her hand. 'Me first! Check this out!'

She tried to neatly fit her piece of the puzzle in with the others but accidently collapsed on top of the clues, spreading the pieces everywhere. She couldn't move at first because she was laughing so hard and trying to apologise at the same time.

'Prani!!'

'S-S-Sorry!'

Many hands tried to help gather the pieces – including the piece they thought they'd lost, but they found clinging to Prani's elbow. When they all settled again, they read the words on her clue:

are invit
day p
y 15 A

'Come on, Phoebe,' Maddy urged. 'Put your piece down.'

Phoebe fit the last piece into the puzzle.

Jump
as your
party?

'Oh my gosh!' screamed Prani. 'We're going to Jump! You know, the trampoline park!' She started bouncing on her knees. 'We're going to Jump! We're going to Jump!' she chanted.

Isabella, Maddy and Sienna joined in, and Jade clapped along. Lily and Charlotte started cheering. 'Yay! Woohoo! I can't *wait*!'

Chapter Twenty-two

Phoebe was as excited as the other girls. It was just becoming real to her that she had actually been invited to a party with her teammates! The whole invitation was clearly written for them all to see.

You birth Sunda	are invit day p y 15 A	ed to arty ugust at	a on 2.00 pm
at Dress Whose	Jump as your party?	M favourit Flip me	arrang. e celebrity. over.

Maddy asked the question they were all thinking. 'This is going to be awesome! But whose party is it?'

Everyone stared at the invitation. Phoebe murmured to herself. 'Flip me over . . . Flip me over . . .' Suddenly, she remembered there was something on the back of each of the puzzle pieces. They'd forgotten the other part of the mystery! Carefully, Phoebe began to flip over the pieces. The other girls immediately caught on and, within seconds, a photo of someone had emerged from the different scraps of colour.

As one, they looked up. Eyes wide in shock, they stared at one girl in particular.

'*Sienna?*'

Sienna grinned back, delighted. Her plan had worked perfectly! No one had suspected her at all!

'Oh my God!'

'What . . .?'

'How . . .?'

'But you got a clue as well!'

Prani threw herself at Sienna, collapsing on top of her. 'You sneaky, sneaky thing!'

Phoebe grinned at Sienna's laughing face.

'Hang on! You told me . . .' began Lily. She pointed her finger at Sienna, pretending to frown. 'I asked you at school about your birthday and you said you weren't having a party!'

Sienna shrugged casually. 'I lied.'

The girls shrieked and laughed and jumped on Sienna. It took them a long time to settle down. They lay sprawled on the grass, all eight of them thinking about what outfit they'd wear to look like their favourite celebrity.

Phoebe was in awe. 'I can't believe I got invited!'

A second later, she realised that she had accidentally spoken aloud! She glanced around in panic.

Lily, who had been lying next to her, sat up. 'Of course you would be invited. You're our netball mate! Oh, and by the way,' Lily continued, 'will you *pleeease* invite me over so we can try out your backyard mini-court together? And then you can come over to my place next!'

Phoebe stared at Lily. She felt the hugest smile spread across her face.

I'm going to a party. I have a new friend. And I'm not so shy anymore!

Player Profile

Phoebe Tadic

Full name: Phoebe Ana Tadic
Nicknames: Phoebs, Zlata ('zlata' means 'golden girl' in Croatian)
Age: 12
Height: 152 centimetres
Family: Mum, Dad and 14-year-old brother, Max
School: Shady Gums College

Hobbies: Phoebe feels like the luckiest girl in the world because she has her very own mini netball court in her backyard! In her free time, Phoebe loves practising her netball skills, especially her goaling. Her favourite people to practise with are her dad; her babysitter, Caitlyn; and her new friend, Lily, who also plays for the Marrang Gems. Phoebe often finds herself daydreaming about being a superstar goal shooter, and although she is shy to admit it, she hopes to one day play for the New Zealand national team, the Silver Ferns. Phoebe relaxes by helping her mum make Kremšnita, her favourite Croatian dessert, which she thinks is the perfect combination of crispy, crunchy pastry and smooth, sweet custard.

Netball club: Marrang Netball Club

Netball team: Marrang Gems, the Marrang Netball Club Under 13s team

Netball coach: Janet

Training day: Wednesday

Netball uniform: Royal blue netball dress with white side panels where 'Marrang' is written in pink. Phoebe likes to wear her long hair in a plait so that it doesn't whip around in the wind and distract her when she plays.

Favourite netball positions: Goal Shooter, Goal Attack

Netball idol: Silver Ferns and Northern Mystics player Maria Tutaia

Best netball moment: Captaining the Gems and throwing a crucial pass which led to the winning goal in the final seconds of their match against the tough Thomson netball team.

Netball ambition: To become a professional netballer and shoot at 100% accuracy for a whole season.

Netball Drills

Balance Practice

1. Gather a set of cones, or any kind of marker.
2. Arrange them on the ground in a straight line so that they are 30 centimetres apart.
3. Start at one end of the line. Make your way to the other end by darting in a zigzag motion around each cone.
4. When you get to the end of the line, do the same on the way back.

HOT TIP
Plant your outside foot on the ground as you dodge. It will keep you balanced.

Be a Stunning Shooter

1. Grab a netball.
2. Stand in front of the goal post and shoot for a goal.
3. If you get the ball through the ring, take one step backwards to increase the challenge, and try shooting again.
4. If you miss, take one step forward so it will be a little easier, and try shooting again.
5. You can increase the challenge even more by stepping backwards and to the side when you get the ball through the ring.

HOT TIP

Count how many goals you get. Keep trying to beat your own score.

Be a Smart Dodger: Leading Out

1. You'll need three people for this drill, as well as a netball.

2. Choose a partner and decide who will be the attacker and who will be the defender. The third person will be holding the ball, ready to pass to the attacker.

3. Draw a line on the ground with some chalk or, if you're at the netball courts, pick one of the transverse lines.

4. The attacker and the defender stand behind the line. The person holding the ball stands in front of the line.

5. When everyone is ready, the person holding the ball calls out for the attacker to run forward. The attacker runs out as fast as they can (this is called 'leading out'), running out wide to the side (either left or right).

6. The attacker quickly changes direction, and runs the other way to take the pass.

7. While the attacker is running, the defender tries to stop the attacker from getting the ball.

8. Swap roles so all three of you can have a go at attacking, defending and passing the ball.

HOT TIP

Change direction really quickly so your defender can't keep up with you!

The Marrang Gems

Maddy Browne
Isabella Contesotto
Sienna Handley
Jade Mathison
Prani Patel
Lily Scott
Charlotte Stevens
Phoebe Tadic

Netball Positions

Position	Full title	Where the player can go	Player's role
WA	Wing Attack	Centre third, your team's goal third but not the goal circle.	To deliver the ball to the GA or GS.
GA	Goal Attack	Centre third, your team's goal third and the goal circle.	To score goals and to help the GS score goals.
GS	Goal Shooter	Your team's goal third and the goal circle.	To score goals and to help the GA score goals.
C	Centre	Everywhere but the goal circles.	To deliver the centre pass. Plays an important role in both attacking and defending down the court.
WD	Wing Defence	Centre third, opposition's goal third but not the goal circle.	To prevent the opposition's WA from getting the ball and to stop them passing it to the GA or GS.
GD	Goal Defence	Centre third, opposition's goal third and the goal circle.	To prevent the opposition's GA from getting the ball and to stop them from scoring a goal.
GK	Goal Keeper	Opposition's goal third and the goal circle.	To prevent the opposition's GS from getting the ball and to stop them from scoring a goal.

OUT NOW

Read ahead for a sneak peek of
Pivot and Win

Chapter One

The Marrang Gems gathered around the seats that lined court one, ready for their Wednesday-afternoon training session. There was lots of chatter – all the girls were friends now, especially after Sienna's fancy-dress birthday party the previous week.

'What's that green thing in your hair, Lily?' asked Maddy. She peered at the back of Lily's head.

'A pipe-cleaner!' Lily replied. She gave the lime-green pipe-cleaner that held up her blonde hair a quick twist.

'Why are you wearing that?' Maddy asked. She laughed at the stiff ends sticking above Lily's head. They looked like little alien antennae.

'Was it for a dare?' asked Prani. She stared with fascination at the makeshift hair tie.

Lily giggled. 'I couldn't find any of my hair ribbons, so I just grabbed this instead. Do you like it?' She twirled in front of the girls so they could all see it.

'Your head looks like a half-finished art project,' said Sienna, grinning. She followed Lily to a space on the netball court for passing practice, whispering to the other girls over her shoulder as she went. 'It's a wonder she can find anything with that mess in her bedroom!'

'Hey, I heard that!' Lily protested.

The other girls laughed. Lily's outrageously messy bedroom was well known.

This was the most familiar part of the Marrang Netball Club Under 13s weekly training session. Their coach, Janet, had them practise each type of pass used in a game of netball. There were chest passes, one-handed passes, bounce passes and high lob passes.

The girls paired up and ran through the first part of training themselves, while Janet stood to one side, talking quietly to Charlotte's mum. Lily loved this drill. It was like memory work for your body.

When they had completed 20 passes of each type, the girls moved to the edge of the court, ready for the next part of training. Eight girls looked at Janet expectantly.

'This week we're going to practise –' Janet frowned slightly, looking at her daughter. 'Lily, what's that on your head?'

'This? It's my hair tie,' said Lily, tilting her head so her mum could see it clearly.

'Why am I not surprised!' said Janet. 'As I was saying . . . Today we're going to practise the pivot. But first I need to see if you remember the stepping rules. How many times can each foot touch the ground before you have to pass the ball? Say it together!'

'Once!' chorused the girls.

'When can that change? Lily?'

'When you keep your landing foot stuck to the ground – then you can move the other foot as much as you like,' Lily answered clearly.

'Well done. What Lily just described is a pivot. Okay, show me a pivot, everyone. Jump forward, making sure you land on one foot first and then the other.' Janet looked around as everyone jumped forward. 'Now point to your landing foot. Charlotte, it's the other one . . . That's it. Now anchor that landing foot to the ground and spin around.'

The girls practised several pivots.

'Great work, girls. I see you can already pivot by taking small steps to change direction.' Janet looked at each girl to make sure they were listening. 'But what about when you need to turn your body really quickly? You might need to pass the ball fast, or spin away from your opponents' arms if they're defending. Then it has to be *one* smooth move – not lots of little ones – so that you can face the opposite way.'

Lily loved the sound of this! She already knew how to pivot, but this was more advanced. It was like a pivot, but . . . better.

'That'd be a *super*-pivot!' she called.

Lily wasn't as timid with Janet as the other girls sometimes were because Janet was Lily's mum. Jade had said at first that Janet would be sure to play favourites because Lily was her daughter, but Janet never did. She was always fair and Lily loved having her as coach. At times she even wondered if the other girls were jealous of her because *her* mum was so good at netball.

Janet grinned at her daughter. 'It *is* like a super-pivot! And it takes practice. We're going to do it in slow motion first. Just like when you learn dance steps, you need to be able to do it slowly before you can do it quickly.'

Chapter Two

Janet turned her back on the team and spoke over her shoulder. 'Watch me first, and then we'll all try the super-pivot.' She began to move really slowly, calling out the movements in a clear voice. 'Catch. Spin. Pass.'

The girls watched her body movement and her footwork several times.

'Now you try it,' said Janet. 'Follow in time with me. Catch. Spin. Pass.'

The team spread out and began to copy Janet.

At first the girls found it difficult to coordinate the movement of their feet and bodies, but like dance steps, it became easier with practice.

Lily noticed that there were different levels of success. Phoebe moved gracefully, like a ballet dancer, but Sienna had a jerky style. Maddy did it perfectly right away, while it took Jade a few tries to get it right because she tended to stomp her foot and bring it down before she had moved the full 180 degrees. Prani, Charlotte and Isabella caught on after a minute or so, but none of them moved as smoothly as Janet.

Once they could pivot quickly, Janet put on some music from her phone playlist. Moving to the fast beat of the top ten songs, the Gems sped up their movements.

Catch. Spin. Pass. Catch. Spin. Pass.

Lily sang along to the songs as she moved, but noticed she was out of step with the other girls. *It's actually easier without music*, she thought. She enjoyed music but always found it hard to find the beat. That's why she had never really liked dancing.

After the final cool-down session, the girls gathered together to grab their water bottles and bags. Lily was still thinking about the super-pivot. 'I'm going to ask my cousin Eliza what she thinks about the super-pivot.'

'Why?' asked Phoebe.

'She's a regional netball talent scout,' said Lily.

Phoebe gasped. 'Seriously?'

'I can't believe you have a cousin who's a talent scout!' said Charlotte.

'Well *my* cousin was on *Big Brother*,' said Jade.

No one acknowledged that old news.

'How come you haven't told us this before, Lily?' asked Phoebe.

'I thought I had,' said Lily. 'My aunt works for Netball Australia as well. She and Eliza know *everyone* in netball.'

'You should get your cousin to come and watch us play. She can talent spot *us*!' said Maddy.

Lily's eyes lit up. 'Yeah, good idea! I can't believe I've never thought of that! I'm seeing her in a few weeks at my aunt's birthday party. Maybe I can ask her about it then.'

Imagine if she saw me play and thought I was good enough to be selected for a state team! Or, one day, the Australian team! Lily was lost in her thoughts for a moment, imagining herself training with the Australian Diamonds. Then she remembered Eliza telling her what the scouts look for in players.

'They need to have the skills but they also need to be tall, Lil, so you'll have to grow a bit!' she had said.

Lily sighed. *Will I ever be tall enough to play? And what about my skills? I'd better work on those!*